THE AUTHOR

Apart from a keen interest in mechanically moving parts, which was in keeping with the inquisitive minds of many young boys, there were no specific characteristic to his unfortunate beginnings. Born Roy Mackpenfield Grant in St Catherine Jamaica, early signs indicated he could have been a gifted child; but, at what?

Though he had many setbacks: the loss of sight in one eye that makes him a disabled person and the loss of a brother he loved; he grew up and become an ambitious and respected individual.

Writing did not play any major role in his young life. The loss of sight in one eye at the age of two years made it difficult for him to focus for long periods. Reading became an exercise that was done on a need to know basis.

What drives his mechanically engineering mind? His mother believed that anything is achievable even when it seemed beyond possibility. Having been the first of eleven children he had his share of disappointments and taunts. But, he progressed into adulthood and was later blessed with five children, one daughter and four sons. Luckily, he has fulfilled most of his dreams and created a legacy that will not to be forgotten; but, could give is family a sense of pride. However, it took an act of total blindness to acknowledge the significance of his achievement and transpire the reality of his dreams to recognise he was born a Gifted Child.

Roy worked for several years as a *Precision Mechanical Engineer: Tool Maker*; as an entrepreneur, he was a taxi Proprietor and had a Mobile Catering Service. He is now volunteering and trustee for many organisations.

BOOKS BY THE SAME AUTHOR

Novels:
When Darkness Turns to Light, 2003 (Reprinted 2010)
Patchwork Culture, 2007
A Mother's Fears, 2010

Plays:
Mama's Kitchen, 2005
Front Room, 2006
Where's Home, 2008
Fruit Fantastic, 2009

Short Stories:
VOL. I: THE INSIDE STORIES
(Selection of Autobiographical Stories)

Magazines:
Nightingales' Stories, 2008
Impatient Society, 2009

To be Published Soon . . .
Happiness Was Their Gold
Journey of Choices
Larry and the Ghost
The Crystal Bowl

A
Mother's Fears

ROY MACKPENFIELD

NEWPORT, WALES
(2010)

Published in 2010 by
MACKPEN BOOKS
E-mail: roy.grant@sewrec.org.uk – roymackpen@aol.com

Roy Mackpenfield
122 Woodside, Duffryn
Newport (South Wales)
NP10 8XE
United Kingdom

ISBN 978-1-907868-00-9

Printed in Wales by
Dinefwr Press
Llandybïe, Carmarthenshire, SA18 3YD

*Dedicated
to furthering the knowledge
of future generations*

Contents

Introduction

The mismanagement of society over the years has created a disabling effect to the stabilising methods of our world and scarred a landscape that is becoming increasingly difficult, for nature to maintain its fine-tuning balance. And, the human race is yet, to perfect a defining rule by which our world could function cohesively. This being the case how do you comfort a disabled child? What could you do or say, when the torture of his or her disability begins to affect the mind and the discomfort it creates become overwhelming? There is no easy answer, more so to those who have not lived that experience.

In a world where the rapid growth of education and technology dominates the agenda, it would be easy to prescribe an antidote that could induce a logical conclusion, perhaps. But, how could anyone be positive that his or her conclusion is the right answer that is without question right for the child? And, could that answer with certainty become the defining path, by which that child is relieved from his or her predicament? The answer in Lafty's case was clouded in uncertainties. His poor and inexperienced mother was powerless to demonstrate the way by which his future could evolve. Like every good parent who strives to provide the best for their child, she too was desperate to secure a path that had fewer obstacles. Unfortunately, she was not equipped with the tools that education provides. But, how could she achieve it? Whatever decision she makes it would have to be in the child's best interest, and even then, she could not be sure it was, what her child wants? Even with verbal communication or, accurate signed interaction, no one could prescribe, with certainty, the correct antidote. So, how could we as parent, pretend to know the answers to the haunting cries, of a distressed child? Using the powers of deduction, the professionals could arbitrate a course of actions, which would enable them to reach a compatible conclusion and in many cases success are attained.

However, there are questions that fall short of a defining answer. Like, how does the success of the professionals affect the mind of a child; does it allow the child to forget his or her disability and set about doing the things that able-bodied children do? Or, is the prescription a hit and miss conjecture. After all, every child is an individual and no two persons are alike. And, every child accepts love and attention, important building blocks in their developing years differently. Loving caring practises are encouraged to invigorate untapped sensors, which could make disabled children susceptible, to adopt and achieve similar results as able-bodies. So, could we with absolute certainty proclaim what is best for a child?

Influential merchants, of the industrial past, used slavery to achieve wealth and broaden their exploitation of a world that is dominated by greed, and created the ugliest humane catastrophe, which is far reaching to any others. Black people from Africa bore the brunt of this treatment than any other human. They were seen as equal to the cattle. Without sense or feeling, they are little differences between them and the plight of a disabled child. Like most or, all disabled persons in the past were locked away, hidden and left to die from their inadequacy. However, slaves could interact with other they were made to work to the last drop of blood and at the same time used to produce the next generation, continuing the cycle until death.

March 2007 marks the bicentennial to the abolition of slavery a significant time for Caribbean slaves. It supposed to represent the abolition of slavery. But, can we take that as gospel? Thank God, at last we have been finally given an audience with the good and the greats, whether or not they listen, it will be left to their consciences.

Grateful though we are, listening to historical news and documentaries and the actions of individuals and organisation more so, of Wilberforce, it would be easy to accept, that the act of abolition of 1807 put an end to slavery and Wilberforce became the liberator. But, it never happened that way, because without the merchants agreement, that act was useless. Furthermore, it took the concretive actions of strong determined slaves and another act of Parliament to give Wilberforce bill power. And, another 32 years for the merchants to concede and accept the act to stop the trafficking of human cargo and speaking of black people in similar terminology as their livestock.

History seems to repeat itself, because throughout this historical rhinestone of abolition, very little emphasis is put on what black slaves did to bring about freedom. As it was, during schooling days, in the homeland, children were denied the facts to their identity and the true history to their ancestries. How much is known about black warriors such as Cudjoe, Nanny, Cuffee, Johnny, Accompong, Cuaco, and many others who won their battle over the British soldiers? All in the name of freedom, those were the real heroes. Not only did they reduce the military might, they hit the British Empire where it hit, its economic structure. Their actions drastically curtail the merchant's wealth, put pressure on them to acknowledge the act, forced them back into the deceit of their accomplices, and commence an end to slavery. In 1838, those warriors signed a treaty with His Majesty King George the second, which gave all the fighting slaves under their control freedom and liberty to live and travel without hindrance. Even though the treaty was signed in 1837, it was not enforced until 1838, which is celebrated on the 6th of January each year by the Maroons and all Jamaicans. This did not represent freedom for all slaves black or otherwise.

Suggestions of retribution have been made, which could be counter productive. Rather than embarking on a path that could create further confusion, let us be positive and move closer, governments and people. Seize this window of opportunity to insist that future generations are given the undiluted history within the educational curriculum. Would not that be a wonderful legacy for future generations to access their identity, through education, learning, and the journey from slavery to freedom? Such developments could also help mothers to understand, more clearly, the source to the cries of a distressed child. And, for those to whom we esteemed, whose power and influence develop the hunger that determined the path by which society is driven, could heed the cries of our disabling world.

CHAPTER 1

Burden of Slavery

In a demanding show of strength, she waited. For three long years she waited for a whisper of news, during which she had blamed herself for what seemed a dreadful decision. The well-trodden ragged roads at every given opportunity scarred her feet as she climbed the winding mountain paths, scaled jagged cliffs, forged the raging rivers and waded through infested swamps to reach the city port. It was the only chance she had to speak to anyone who might know the man who took her son to a distant land. But her journey was fruitless and ended in vain. No one knew, neither the man nor the son she sought. Tears flooded her sleepless nights, as she wondered if he had lived or died. She struggled to survive the darkness, but came alive with the dawning sun. Its brightening rays gave her hope and strengthened her determined attitude to search once more. Marybell had suffered society's exploits and was powerless to change what nature seemed to have ignored.

Her family lived and worked on the great slave plantation. One of four children, Marybell was brought up with a group of families who lived as one unit, all sharing similar circumstances, destined to increase the slave population. They were seen as little more than domestic servants and breeding machines. They shared the same poor standards, a lifestyle dictated by the masters who provided dwellings that were too small to accommodate the large families they were expected to produce; a deliberate practice that demonstrated their worth. Many of their offspring were in fact blood-related, with one common bond: they were slaves or treated as slaves with no identity other than that they were from a distant land and their future was at the mercy of their master's whim.

Marybell's childhood was determined by the rule of the great household, which was unwavering hard work. She grew up anchored by one focal denominator, to serve and obey. Her life was controlled by the rules. Having been born into an oppressive system in which society demanded she did not have a choice, her life was set on a collision course that disrupted those delicate childhood years. When she should have been experiencing the joys of growing up, the system was drastically altering her future. Slavery had created a nation reduced to apathy, led by faults, smiles and selfish cultures. It was not a mother's wish to see her child condemned to a life of hopelessness, which made the burden of slavery as devastating as the cries of a disabled child.

It all started at the tender age of twelve, by which time her beautifully sculptured personality, her long, black straight hair, her light complexion and skin as smooth as velvet indicated she was of mixed parentage. Even though slaves like her were given limited freedom to manage their lives, in part they stayed loyal to their masters. It could have been said that he was a good master. But was he?

Living in West Virginia he was said to be a good Christian person. He treated his slaves well and they loved him. But they kept asking him where they came from. Where was home? One day the master looked across his vast fields to an enormous lake, and said, 'Can you see that massive lake of water? You came from there.' The poor slaves were very pleased with his explanation. 'At last,' they said, 'we belong somewhere. Hurray, one day we can return home.' Nothing more was said and the happy smiling slaves went about their business.

The following day, the slave master awoke to a beautiful sunny sky. Induced by the fragrant, budding flowers of the water lilies, swarms of bees, butterflies and colourful, humming doctor birds competed for its tasty nectar. Happy to be alive and able to enjoy his achievement, he took his usual morning ride along the lakeside. Halfway, he stopped and gazed across the richness of a fertile land, with fields of wealth-bearing crops and a sea of water that hosted a multitude of colourful birds. They were diving, swimming, feeding and pluming their feathers, a spectacular sight to behold. Enchanted by this beauty, he scanned the water and his eyes spotted something floating, something bigger than any of those birds. Curious, he took a closer look. As his focus sharpened, he soon realised it was a body. The shock sent him and his horse galloping off to fetch his manservant. On their return, his manservant got into a boat and rowed out to the body. But it wasn't just one body they found, there were three bodies floating on the water. The slave master was stunned and could not understand why they were there. But the night after he had told the slaves where they came from, three of them had gone in search of the pathway to their ancestral home and in the process drowned. So the question is, was he as good a person as he made believe?

In every family there is always one who goes the opposite way and Marybell's mother was that person; she chose to walk away from her family and went in search of a future of her own making. But there were pitfalls in this path and Marybell's mother wasn't immune to those dangers. In her quest to find a different future to that of her parents, she met Marybell's father. The experience left her with four children and no steady income, and forced her to make decisions that shrouded Marybell's life, landing her in a world of uncertainties and mistrust. Her world became an endless chain of hardships, and Marybell's mother was forced to give her daughter away in the hope that the other children could survive, shattering Marybell's innocent childhood at a most crucial time, at the age of twelve. She was given away like an unwanted kitten to an aunt, who treated her very badly. She was a wicked aunt, whose indiscretions caused Marybell's uncle to remove her and take her into his own already overcrowded home.

With no strong parenting Marybell became a loose cannon and her life took an unfortunate twist. She was fast approaching the ideal age for marriage and was the perfect target for Ruben, a sailor who had spotted her during one of his many trips to the island. It was an opportunity for him to make what he wanted of this young hardworking slave child. He was thankful for her uncle's decision to remove her from her cruel aunt as it gave him the chance he had been waiting for to charm this innocent, vulnerable girl, to promise her the kind of friendship she was yet to experience, to promise her freedom and happiness. She was quickly swept off her feet and Ruben became a sort of saviour in her eyes. She was a beautiful young girl, but naïve. She had taken her uncle's kindness for granted and interpreted Ruben's smiling face as truthful and honest, with no other motives. But Marybell was wrong. She was wrong because within a few months of meeting Ruben his smile had claimed her virginity, and she discovered she was pregnant. She was young, too young to be a match for Ruben's overwhelming charms, which sowed feelings of love that clouded her judgement. Cloaked in happiness, she could think of none other than Ruben. She was also convinced that Ruben had similar feelings and could only see a long-term relationship with him.

After meeting Marybell, Ruben gave up going to sea and stayed with her during her pregnancy. His presence gave her confidence and strengthened his hold on her, and she rejected the advice of her worried uncle that their home was too small to accommodate another person, let alone a newborn child.

The house was a small, round, single room building. Its neatly thatched roof, a mixture of mud and straw which sealed the wattle walls, made the building warm in the nights and cool during the hot days, but it was already too small for Marybell's uncle family. Everyone predicted that this love match was unhealthy, and Ruben would eventually break her heart. But Marybell was in love; her faith in Ruben was too strong to get broken. She could not see anything wrong in what she was doing and felt sure Ruben would stay with her for life; not necessary in that house. One day they would build a home of their own and continue to raise their family.

At sixteen, Marybell was far too young and inexperienced to grasp the implications of her wishes and the heartbreak that might result if their love match turned sour. Though she wasn't a physically disabled person, the world in which she lived made her disabled. She could recite the alphabet in part, but was unable to read or write a sentence. However, she had a formidable capacity to love and care for those around her. Some said it was a gift. Maybe that was why she failed to understand that her desire to raise a family with Ruben might one day cause her dreams to be shattered.

Against the negative flow of opinion, Marybell gave birth to a son and they named him Lafty. His arrival made her the happiest person in the world, fulfilling her dreams. It forced her to take on all the responsibilities of motherhood that she did not then realise would in time become a burden for her to have to carry out alone.

She had given birth to a disabled child. At first, they did not know and could not understand his symptoms, but that did not stop them showering the boy with the love and attention which helped him grow up accepting his disability. There were times, however, when he became confused by a fear of indifference. Excellent though their caring was, it did not change the way in which others saw him. He would always be a disabled person with something missing – he was incomplete, they said. The happiness of a loving boy with many friends, and a father who was close to his family, made the relationship blossom, and it wasn't long before Marybell fell pregnant for a second time and gave birth to a sister for Lafty, a daughter to complete Marybell's wishes. But time was against Marybell and it seemed her family's warnings were about to bear fruit. She had become a single parent with two children and no help from the father she had hoped would be there for her.

This new development made providing for her children's needs seem impossible. Like many of the slave children on the plantation, they were denied the right to an education. Marybell's generation did not have any rights, their duty was to serve in whatever capacity they were suited, which put Lafty and his sister at a disadvantage from the day they were born. It was at times like these, when confusion created havoc in Lafty's already disturbed mind, that the struggle of bringing up two children overwhelmed her. Her son had reached the age of twelve – the age at which she had been given to her aunt for a better chance in life – and was growing up without an education. Marybell needed help, the kind that could give her children a better future. She wanted to save her children from being a slave child like she had been, before their chance of enjoying their childhood slipped away.

Poor and helpless as she was, there was no easy solution and her children seemed destined to a future she could not change. She was desperate, so desperate that she began to pray for any opportunity to alter their destiny. Time was fast running out on the hope she harboured for her twelve-year-old son, Lafty. She did not want history to repeat itself but soon she would no longer be able to protect him from what seemed a foregone conclusion. Boys of his age were taken from their homes and put to work in conditions that invariably led to an early death, a prospect that haunted her deeply.

Whether it was the sign she had been waiting for, that her prayers were being answered, or whether it was just sheer coincidence, Ruben unexpectedly reappeared. She was very happy to see him, and for a moment forgave him for leaving her with false hopes and promises. He did not know what was going on in her mind. All he wanted was to get back into her good books, so he was quick to take advantage of her weakness. He suggested that he took Lafty away to live with a rich aunt on another island in the Caribbean. He must have been reading my mind, Marybell thought. It was just the opportunity she had hoped for. She wanted a family or someone that would understand her son's needs, someone who would protect him and free him from the pits of slavish conditions. Ruben was a Godsend, she thought. He had brought the answer to her fears, how could she ignore him? But how could she make a twelve-year-old boy understand that her intentions were in his best interests? She knew there and then that her decision could have a devastating effect on Lafty's life. She also knew that Lafty would not want to be separated from her and his sister, because he had a loving home that he adored. Furthermore, he knew very little of his father, not enough to leave his home, however poor it was, to live with him. At twelve, he was in no position to argue for his future. Lafty had been born with a speech impediment and had difficulty in expressing himself. He had a low standard of educational capability and was shackled to the rules of his mother, who wanted to spare him from the awful and unforgiving slurs of able-bodied people. He had already endured eight relenting years of taunts, thought Marybell, not to mention the stigma of not having a father to comfort the hurt he had felt. His dreams of growing up with his sister and friends in the environment he loved would be shattered. Though he was in no position to disapprove, she wondered how she could tell him. Whatever happened, she thought, she was determined to do everything she could to safe him from a future of slavery.

The dust of one windswept day had barely settled, with fallen leaves covering every inch of open space, when the red evening sun slipped beneath the horizon while Marybell and Ruben sat beneath a mango tree. Transfixed by her thoughts, her eyes stared beyond the clouds as though someone was there in the shadows speaking to her. Could it have been Ruben's voice she heard? Lafty walked towards her, crushed leaves crackling beneath his shoeless feet, causing her lips to part in a smile. She wanted to embrace the son she loved. He was aglow in happiness reminding her of those years when his father was living at home, and told stories of his family. They had been happy times with memories that made her present situation so much more difficult than she had expected. Ruben had told her that Lafty's grandfather was a slave child, and had grown up in very fortunate position. He had been given an education that helped him to carve out a position of respect for himself within the communities. He had been able to make choices from an early age, and this had allowed him to become a feared individual. He had also been a very handsome man, loved by the ladies. As he befriended as many women as he could, some said his grandfather was a ram let loose among the ewes. His conquests resulted in the birth of many children. No one knew for sure how many children had been named after him or had carried the plantation's name. And, with arrogance, Ruben told her, 'My father did not see the need to respect or honour his fatherly responsibilities.'

Like his father, Ruben was a chip off the old block. He, too, paid little or no attention to the responsibility of his children. He was a handsome fellow, probably like his father, tall, with an athletic physique and fair skin. His well-sculptured body and ocean blue eyes made him an attractive specimen, which was unusual for a black man. He had an irresistible charm that was particularly alluring to ladies. Marybell was no exception, she fell hook, line and sinker to Ruben's charm. He was her first love; to her he was everything and nothing else mattered. But they did not live together for as long as she had hoped, because Ruben went back to work, sailing between the Caribbean islands and Panama. For him it was the ideal opportunity to spread his charms among the islanders wherever he went. There were many who had fallen victim to his romantic escapades, and 15 children, all told, that resulted. But Ruben would always revisit his old conquests from time to time, even though it was often many years between visits.

CHAPTER 2

Greatest Decision

Ruben was confronted with the plight of his children and their mother's desperate needs. The situation had turned to his advantage and his hopes of making peace were alive. Marybell was forced to break her golden rule, and send her son to play out of earshot so that she could talk privately with his father. She needed the space to convince Ruben of his responsibility to the children, to give her peace of mind and help secure the future she wanted for their son. She thought it was time that he made some contribution to the care of his son and daughter, Lafty and Celene. But her greatest concern was that of their son Lafty. He was at that crucial age when he could be taken away by the master or an elder and either sold or put into one of the plantation households where he would be slavishly treated, regardless of his disability. She had seen what slavery did to her parents and grandparents; even to her, albeit for a short time, a prospect from which she hoped to save her child.

Ruben's arrival brought relief to her stricken heart. A travelling man with a large family dotted across the islands, she felt convinced that he would have the answer to her fears. In desperation she poured out her worries to Ruben, which was music to his ears. He had heard it all before, and on many occasions, but this time the tune was much more engaging.

She was prepared to sacrifice her strength to this philanderer who seemed to have the answer. Ruben had a big wealthy family, she thought. Surely he would not lie about his rich sister? She might be the answer, the one who might gladly adopt her twelve-year-old boy as a son or nephew and give him an education. Having heard her plea, Ruben knew that the mother of his son would do anything for his help, and, without effort, he slipped his charm into gear. He became a man of means, who could take care of his son, even though for eight years he had failed miserably. Clinging to hope, Lafty's mother listened to Ruben's grand plan for her son. It was true that Ruben had several brothers and sisters dotted across the islands, and, more importantly, that they all had positions of wealth. She knew that Ruben's father was from a wealthy family, so she did not need much convincing of his family's capability to care for her son. But, she wondered, why is he so happy to help after all these years?

Whatever his motives were for her son there were no alternatives. Either he went to work for his family or became a slave for the oppressors. Ruben's charm had reassured her that he would take Lafty to live with his aunt, who would make sure the boy had an education and a secure future away from slavery. Furthermore, he would be at hand to make sure that their son was brought up within a happy environment. Ruben realised that his infrequent visits would become more welcome if Lafty was placed with some-one many miles away from Marybell, and that his sister was in fact wealthy, and could adequately care for Lafty.

However, Ruben's sister had neither seen nor heard of Lafty, Lafty's sister, or of Marybell. In truth Ruben was unconcerned with the boy's welfare and was probably only trying to secure a bed for himself when he was in town. Lafty's plight had presented him with an opportunity to put into action one of his many half-baked ideas that seemed, at face value, the perfect remedy to Marybell's problem. Although their plan for Lafty seemed promising, there was one nagging question. How could she be parted from her son? Tears trickled down her cheeks as the protective fears of motherhood overwhelmed her emotions. But Ruben's smooth talk slowly melted the doubts from her mind and left his ideas as the only credible solution.

Lafty had come alive, excited at the arrival of his Ruben. He had seen very little of him during his twelve years and was itching to ignite the bond he had built up in his mind as his father's irregular visits had not given them time to bond. This time, Lafty thought, they would get to know each other. But Ruben was not as keen, because he was preoccupied talking to Marybell and could not pay Lafty the attention that the boy wanted. Lafty also had all sorts of questions for his father. Is my father trying to avoid me? he wondered. He was keyed up to know more about his father and wanted a story he could share with his friends, a story he could be proud to repeat, that would boost his confidence and release his isolated spirit, placing him squarely with those friends who had fathers at home. The story of his journey, his ship, how many sailors lived on it, what countries they visited and what the people were like in those countries. Were they the same? Not an unreasonable request, you might think, for a young boy with an inquisitive mind. But he did not get the chance to ask his father any of these burning questions.

Ruben was busily locked in conversation with Marybell and was dismissive of Lafty's presence, which convinced the boy that something was not quite right. Though he was twelve, he felt sure that his parents' dismissive actions had something to do with his future. Worried that he might have done something wrong and was about to be punished, the little boy tried desperately to hear what was being said. Unfortunately he could not get close enough, and there was no other way of knowing what they were planning. To make matters worse he could see tears on his mother's cheeks. And that seemed to seal it; he did not know what to do next. He felt like running away, but where would he go? If he ran away and his mother could not find him, he thought, that would make things even worse than they already were. There was nowhere to hide in the community, because everyone looked out for each other and if he got caught, he could be disciplined by any of the elders. So it would be pointless doing anything silly and inflaming a delicate situation. He knew the hardship his mother faced, providing a roof over their heads and putting food on the table. From a distance he became more and more distraught as he watched the changing expressions on her face, and the erratic movements of her head and hands, which suggested she was agitated. Sadness shadowed his mind as he tried to make sense of what was going on. If he could only hear what they were saying, he thought, it would make it much easier to understand the way an adult thought. What could be so bad, he wondered, as to put his mother on a knife-edge with worry? He wanted to hug and tell her how much he loved her but there was nothing he could do but wait.

While Lafty sat feeling sorry for himself, Marybell was well aware what might be going on in her son's head, because she, too, had had a similar experience at his age. Her parents had had to take a decision of epic proportions, and all the signs pointed to the inevitability of her doing the same, if not that day then another day, sooner than later. But Marybell wanted an assurance that her son was not going to fall into the same trap. Again and again the same question kept popping into her head. How could I ever be sure? The cruel answer was that she never could be.

While Lafty waited in silence, Ruben was extremely pleased with himself. He was closer to Marybell than at any other time during the last eight years. Like a wounded animal Marybell curled up beside him, desperate to hear those words that would spell out the right answers. She was at her lowest ebb with worry which made her vulnerable and prime for exploitation. She needed help in making that decision, but all she had was the man she wanted to hate. Marybell had turned to her last source of help. But was he a changed man that could be trusted? Memories of Ruben's past flooded her head. His constant flipping in and out of her life like a bee to the honeycomb was not the life she had expected. He was very good at making lavish promises. It was easy for him, he had an education – something she had aspired to. But he had also promised to teach her how to read and write properly, another promise he had failed to fulfil. She had to conceive of Ruben as a selfish person, who put himself first and was there to take advantage of those qualities she possessed.

Lafty's predicament had highlighted a lot of Ruben's shortcomings. It became clear to her than that Ruben had pulled off a masterstroke in making her the mother of his children and putting an end to the educational help he had promised. But she loved him and would always have a tender spot for this Romeo, to the extent that she tried to justify his actions by blaming the jobs he had had to take. She even made herself believe that it was his travelling to find work that had put a stop to her education and opened the gap in their relationship. But how could she justify that first journey to sea that had lasted two years? On his return Lafty had reached the age of four and his development had even then been causing concerns. He could not walk nor could he speak with any clarity. He communicated through weird sounds and gestures. Only Marybell's motherly instinct had enabled her to understand his needs. It was at times such as those that she had needed Ruben's presence, to share her thoughts and doubts with him, but his infrequent visits did not gave her the time to discuss her fears. Every time he came home and went away again he always told her that they would find the time to talk on his next visit. But time was running out fast and Lafty was getting older with no sign of improvement. The childish taunts and pranks were beginning to affect his behaviour, while the gap between his father's visits stretched from months to years, leaving her the burden of long nights and the emptiness of waiting for the man she loved, suffering the hardship of bringing up two children without a father or a steady income. But despite all of this she had always remained hopeful that he would come back to her.

This time she thought things were going to be different. It's decision time, she told herself. Lafty's future is at stake. For too long Ruben has failed to pay attention to his son's disability. It was time he lived up to his fatherly responsibility and secured a place, or help, for him somewhere he would not be subjected to slavery. Marybell was determined, though desperate, to trust Ruben again, because not everything he had told her in the past had been false. It was his irresponsible attitude that gave her cause to hesitate.

She hugged him while the sun slipped its moorings and dipped over the hill tops and the cool evening breeze brought an air of calm that filtered through her soul, igniting ripples of romance across her body. His closeness and the feel of his muscles sent a tingling sensation through her veins, creating an uncontrollable surge of emotion, with a compelling effect. Marybell agreed to Ruben's suggestion. And for the first time since his arrival, she felt as free as the birds, and her face oozed happiness. Ruben's assurances had removed her nagging feelings of guilt. The possibility of her son leading a life of slavery had slowly dispersed, leaving her soul filled with joyful belief. His smooth talking seemed to have paid off. She knew there may have been other plans on his mind, but if there were then there was very little else she could do, because she did not have the ability to further examine his motives. His superior intelligence had drowned her simple thoughts. After all, she was illiterate. She was driven by fears that made her desperate to find a solution to her son's needs, and trust became her only choice. Having discovered her weakness, Ruben was quick to revel in the wit of his charm, and was free to make his final move and claim his conquest.

A life spent sailing an ocean basted in beautiful sunshine, awash with fresh tropical breezes, had been the ideal prescription for his bronzed skin and rippling muscles, qualities that sparked an attraction in the eyes of every lady he met. Marybell had succumbed to those temptations many years ago and had tried to dismiss them as memories on many occasions. However, the gentle touch of his warm hands hugging her fragile body, and the feel of his muscles set her eyes ablaze and sent her heart pumping at a rapid rate. Mindful of the past, she became transfixed with thoughts of those powerful muscles battling the dangers of a fearless sea, and for a moment her body turned into a wishing well. The long days of worrying had taken their toll, and left her drained; too weak to care. Helpless against the strength of Ruben's whims, she had caved in and decided that Lafty would go with his father.

Ruben's scheming had paid off, with only the darkened sky a witness his deeds. Marybell had exhausted every opportunity open to her, and was satisfied that Ruben would fulfil his commitment. She felt relieved and could only pray that she had secured the future she wanted for her son, that the decision she had made was the right one. All that was left was to prepare Lafty for the journey.

Lafty was oblivious to what was going on. Even though he had tried to eavesdrop on what was being said he had been forced to play away from their ears, allowing them the space to talk in private. Having been the eldest and only boy child, Lafty had enjoyed a wonderfully close relationship with his mother and sister. Though he was a disabled child, he had a happy and content attitude that had encouraged Marybell to find work where she could, while he and his sister were under to the watchful eyes of her friends and families. So, it was only natural that they had formed an extremely close bond. Marybell had given her children the one thing she knew best, love and care. But to do that, she had had to take work wherever and whenever she could. She had not liked leaving her responsibility to others, it was difficult, but that had been the reality of her life.

Marybell was also a great believer in teaching respect, and had been happy to pass that knowledge on to the children, knowing it would be of great value during their childhood years. They had been taught how to love and care for each other. However, the cost of caring for those children had been getting steadily greater by the day, and to make matters worse her earnings could not match it. But how could she explain her predicament to those children?

Having had similar experiences, Marybell was aware of her son's feelings, and how he would react when told, and this haunted her. But what, she wondered, could she have done differently? As far as she was concerned, sending Lafty to an aunt neither he nor she had ever met was better than allowing him to drift into child slavery.

The gathering clouds obscured the smiling moon, leaving the dimly lit twinkling stars looking on. The brightening eyes of the night-flies sparkled as echoes of the night set the darkness alive. It was time for bed and the little boy was yet to make a fuss of his father. Ruben had been too busy repairing his wayward past and securing an easy access to Marybell's affections. Lafty was Ruben's son, but did he know the child? He might have been there during the first two years of the child's life, but what about those ten missing years? Was his son's future his priority? Was the promise he made to Marybell sincere? His record did not bear much scrutiny. He was happy, and so he should have been. His plan had succeeded and he and his son would set off early the following morning to an undetermined destination in one of the many islands in the Caribbean Sea.

CHAPTER 3

The Nightmare

With tearful eyes and a reluctant mind, Marybell busily gathered together the few pieces of clothing Lafty possessed. Neatly she folded them, and piece by piece she tidily wrapped them into a brown paper parcel. But her breathing had become a rasping and the crackling noise of the wrapping paper gave the impression that she was angry. A single room house was not the right environment for a twelve-year-old boy. Its thin cloth screen afforded no privacy to its inhabitants, and the children could hear and see everything that went on in that house. The strange noise became a concern to Lafty as she continued her preparations and for a moment both children thought their mother was choking. Little did they know that it was the sound of confusion. As they were happy children who took their places among the clutter of an overcrowded house with its crudely built bed against an almost transparent wall, they were not ready to complain. But their little hearts were in turmoil and they did not know what to think. Shrouded in sadness and confusion, they became emotionally charged, awash with tears. Lafty and his sister needed a comforting answer. First they thought their mother was going away; leaving them with a father they barely knew. Then they thought they were the ones that were being sent away. Their own breathing became erratic, and their queasy breath caught Marybell's attention. She pulled back the thin screen, squeezed her way to their bedside and was shocked by the torrent of tears that flooded their faces. Worried and bemused she sat beside them, held them one in each arm, and gently stroked their shivering bodies. Their hearts beat uncontrollably against her body.

The love of those children was of paramount importance, and their breaking down was not a good sign. They must have taken her conversation with Ruben more seriously than she had expected. But how could she gain the assurance she badly needed from the man she doubted? It was time that she faced that daunting fact, she thought. Throughout that day Marybell had tried desperately to hide her emotion from the children without success, but they had become more upset than she feared. How can I tell my children the truth, she wondered; what will they think of me as a mother? Lafty and his sister Celene were too young to understand the complicity of adults. Repeatedly Marybell kissed her children, reassuring them that everything would be all right and there was nothing for them to worry about.

'Why are you two crying?' she asked.

The sobbing children could not answer. They were afraid to reveal what was going in their minds in case their mother was upset. They were good and obedient children and complaining would give the impression that they were naughty. Furthermore, it would be wrong to ask questions they were not supposed to ask. Lafty and Celene. were children, and it would be rude if their mother thought they had been listening to adult conversation.

It was important that Marybell maintained their innocence. But however painful it might have been for her, she had to come clean and give an acceptable reason for her behaviour. She had to think quickly and avoid misleading them; give them an answer of partial truth about the discussion she had had with their father. Her heart was full to bursting; her lips quivered with emotion knowing she could not tell her children the whole truth.

'Lafty, your father is here to take you on a long journey to visit his aunt. You will travel on his ship and you will have a whale of a time sailing the sea. Do you remember when we used to sit and watch the yellow sun slipping beneath the sea and you used to get excited and talk about sailing on one of those ships we saw in the harbour, just like your father's? Well, the time as come.'

Lafty's face came alive with a smile from ear to ear as if to say, 'Now?'

'Not tonight, son, tomorrow. I'm sure you'll enjoy it. Cheer up; you'll get what you've always wanted. Don't worry; you'll be back in no time. And, we'll be waiting for you.'

The little boy dried his tears and made a muffled sound as he tightened his grip, as if to say, 'That is great.' Slowly his heartbeat was as calm as the flat sea, and thoughts of adventure flooded his mind. Captivated by this joyful news, his brain was released from the pain of worrying. He was not unduly worried that his sister could become lonely because, he thought, she was too young, and furthermore, girls were not allowed to go sailing. There were no spoken words but Marybell felt relieved by his calmness, which suggested he understood her thoughts. His relaxed composure left her feeling pleased that her decision could have been the right one. But thoughts that she might probably never see her son again became a raging fire burning away on the inside.

'No more talking now. Hush,' she whispered, and gently tucked them up in bed. She pulled back the screen and walked back to where Ruben patiently sat listening with interest to all that was being said. But the burden of truth weighed heavily on her mind, that the man she once loved had overwhelmed her heart, perhaps enough for her to mislead her children.

Marybell was too trusting for her own good. She was too quick to put aside those lonely days of suffering when Ruben should have been there to help her. Instead, she was ready to latch onto those rare moments of his arrival, when he would do nothing else but spin her bucket full of excuses for his absence. It was hard to believe that true love was the reason for her attraction to him. Had she confused true love with lust for the beauty of his physical appearance? There is no denying that he was a very attractive man, handsome one might say. With his physique it was understandable that her brain turned into a bucket of dysfunctional jelly in his presence.

In silent thought she sat and wondered how her family and friends would react when the news of her decision filtered through. It would be sure to create misgivings. They might think she was going mad and set off a trail of whispers of accusation and blame. Like petals falling off a flowering rose, they might talk in clusters about the girl they loved and respected, but would they try to understand the reasoning for the catastrophic decision she had taken? Would they listen before they laid blame and judged her a wicked person? Hopefully someone would take sympathy with her plight and respect the wishes she cherished for her son.

The pain of her silent thoughts began to erode Ruben's brain, sending nervous twitches through his body. Having stayed away for so long he had no idea of the tremendous bond that existed between mother and son. His ignorance could be forgiven, after all he had never stayed in one place long enough to bond with anyone. But the mother of his children had a special connection between her son and daughter, which she clearly had hoped would stay that way.

Marybell got up from beside Ruben and blew out the light of the tiny oil lamp that sat on a table near to the door. The sudden darkness invited the dim light of the moon through a crack in the mud-straw walls and gave her hope as she undressed. Her thoughts flooded with questions she could not answer. Let's run through it one more time, she thought. His clothes are packed; shoes polished to a shine. I have done it all, there is nothing more I can do, but what if I am wrong? She was not exactly beaming with happiness; her movements were those of a worried person about to cry. Ruben became concerned and held her firmly against his bulging muscles.

'I love you, Marybell. Be strong for our son Lafty,' he whispered. The softness of his voice soon ignited a flame under those words and rekindled the love she once esteemed, adding strength to the decision she had made. They both lay on the tiny bed that was only big enough for one person, and yet on which the two of them lay in comfort while the darkness took control. Emotionally charged by his presence, Marybell could not sleep. Ruben, however, drifted away.

Whoever said the night was a quiet time, thought Marybell. It may be for some, but for her it was the opposite. Like the noise of the restless night creatures she could hear around her, her thoughts buzzed with riddles until the impeccable clockwork brain of a cockerel signalled an end to the night time. But while the cockerel bird was at ease as it crowed the arrival of the morning on which Ruben and Lafty would depart on a ship that would not wait, Marybell was still on edge. Such crowing formed no part of her plans. After a sleepless night the intimidating light of the encroaching dawn made her weak and helpless. But whether or not she had slept she had duties to perform, so she rose to her feet with no thoughts of tomorrow, only of today. Her stomach would be empty when her son disappeared. Her soul feared losing her son but it was too late to change what seemed destined. Spurred by a voice to stick to her decision, she cried, 'Wake up. You must go now. The ship's anchor is about to be lifted.'

Frightened from his sleep, Ruben shouted, 'Where's my boy?'

'He is ready and waiting, so don't you fret.'

The morning sun greeted Marybell's swollen eyes as if there was something it wanted to say. With slumbering thoughts she packed and cleared away the doubting cobwebs of yesterday. It was time for them to leave so she hugged her son and kissed him goodbye. With tear-filled eyes she told Ruben, 'Lafty is my man, with thoughts and fears just like me.' Her words made Celene cry uncontrollably, and while gathering families and friends looked on, no one other than her uncle knew there was a chance that Lafty might not return to the home he loved.

The speed at which they had awoken suggested that any overnight contemplation had cleared, and that some sort of mechanical motion was in control. Marybell's eyes were dry, but it was not so for Lafty. He did not want to go, and seemed to have had a change of heart. He woke feeling rejected by the mother he loved. She tried to talk to him and bring some comfort to his distraught mind, telling him how important he was to her, but nothing she said could make Lafty feel as safe with his father as he had been with her.

It was time for Marybell, Celene, and a gathering crowd of people to walk Lafty, that most precious cargo, to the bus-cart, but Marybell's feet had other ideas and seemed to reject her commands, becoming heavier with every step. The stop for the bus-cart was approximately two hundred yards away; a relatively short distance that became the longest walk for Marybell. Even the narrow pathway appeared to register an objection to her persisting footsteps, while the drizzling rain obscured her vision, filling the potholes that threatened to swamp her feet. Nothing or no one wanted to see Lafty leave. From the gathering crowd there were cries of 'Good luck, Lafty. Have a good trip and don't forget to enjoy your stay,' and 'Bring something back for me.' But few of them knew that this was probably the last time they would see their friend Lafty, even though the atmosphere was more that of a funeral march than a boy being taken on an adventure trip.

Horses and carts, bicycles and people turned the place into something like a Christmas fare. But while most twelve-year-olds would find the prospect of travelling very exciting, Lafty did not. He was wailing, breaking his heart, and could think of nothing other than the presence of his mother and sister. He was creating feelings of embarrassment for his father.

Discipline is crucial in the lives of young and old, more so to a growing lad, and its practices take many forms. A child crying in public was not tolerated; it sent out the wrong message about his or her parents, and Lafty's behaviour might have been regarded as unruly. His continuous crying became a humiliation for Ruben, suggesting that he was being brutal, that Lafty was in danger or at worst that he was being kidnapped. Fearful of what others might think, Ruben could not punish the lad. The boy was doing nothing wrong. Comforting words were his only option and he was forced to fall back on his charm to bring a warm, inviting smile to Lafty's face. It helped to distract onlookers from his dilemma.

They boarded the bus-cart in which the crowd were squashed into seats like pickling bowls. The driver slashed his whip and the four giant horses took up the strain. Slowly the wooden cart began to move as the massive hooves of longhaired horses gripped the rough gravel-covered road and effortlessly pulled the cart. Echoes of crunching loose stones beneath the wheels encouraged the horses' quickening steps. High above, the brightening sun ignited the smells of rotting vegetation, of horses' and other animals' discharge that littered the narrow streets. The rocking, clanging cartwheels bumped along the uneven dusty road, making Lafty's head dizzy and setting off a rumbling in his stomach. There were people of all shapes and sizes moving in all directions. Some neatly dressed, others in rags; all expressing moods of self satisfaction, and all rushing but getting nowhere fast. The crowded road put his frightened mind on a collision course with his father's. For Lafty it was a terrifying experience he could hardly forget. Thank goodness they had no further than two miles to travel and that there was something new and eye-catching to occupy his twelve-year-old thoughts around every turn.

Finally the horses stopped, their journey to the waiting ship at an end. The wooden cart door swung open with a squeal, as if someone was in pain.

'Come along,' a gentle voice whispered, but Lafty's knees were shaking and he could not stand straight without the help of his father's out-stretched hands. 'Hold on to me', he said. Lafty held his father's hands and nervously stepped from the cart, but an ocean of faces of different shapes and sizes and teeth like elephant tusks scared him more. The little boy was clearly traumatised by this new experience. But he firmly held his brown paper parcel and obediently followed his father's footsteps. Standing tall beside the father he loved, Lafty became excited, mesmerised even. He was within touching distance of this magnificent vessel and was about to share its glory. It dwarfed the tiny harbour. Its giant mass reached out into the sky, making the ship the biggest thing he'd ever seen. And all those men with huge muscles just like his father, working in groups, busily carrying on their backs heavy loads of all descriptions, loading the massive ship. The gangway, packed to bursting as people made their way up the narrow steps, shook like a dancing puppet. He was too excited to care. The heat of the morning sun reminded them where they were; a hot country where the sun always shines.

The joys of boarding a ship of that size captured the little boy's mind and injected a smile into every step as he climbed. It was hard to believe what was happening to him, but it was reality and he was not dreaming. Suddenly his racing heart came to a stop as he faced the man at the desk dressed like a captain, an official of a sort who asked his name. Ruben quickly answered, 'He's my boy – Lafty.' The man then stamped his piece of paper and gave Lafty a friendly grin, but his twisted face made Lafty laugh, and for the first time in two days Lafty made Ruben smile. At last Ruben thought his plans were about to come together. Lafty was showing signs of being a happy boy, which was good. After all, he told himself, I want him to be happy when I present him to my sister. Ruben himself had no luggage, he was going back to work and only had to sign in and wait to start his working shift.

They both made their way down the steps along a narrow gangway, where the heat and smells irritated Lafty's throat. He could hear the noise of the engine sounding like a jackhammer thumping through the walls. I'll probably suffocate if we stay here long, he thought. Encouraged by his father, Lafty hurriedly followed. He was anxious to know how much further they had to go but couldn't ask his father, so he kept his silence. Soon they reached a tiny door that bore a familiar landmark, a pair of long rustic handles that had special significance in his memory as they were replicas of the handles on the gates of the plantation house. The doorway offered just enough room for one person to enter or leave. His thoughts were twisted with questions he could not answer but dared not ask his father, like what if this cabin should get flooded, how would we get out? He was not sure if the walls were made of wood or steel. One thing he was sure of, there were no opening windows for them to escape. Fresh air seemed a rationed commodity that was served on request by the opened decks. So if a storm should develop and engulf the ship we would suffocate or drown, he thought. But his love of ships and the adventures of travel dismissed the maybes from his mind and coaxed his acceptance of this adventure, which after all did not seem such a bad idea. And yet his young mind could not escape the confusion of that eventful day. Ruben could smile. He was the happiest one, because everything seemed to be going in his favour. After all, his plan was off to a flying start. He had been given permission to take his son on board, and his workmates had already agreed to help in caring for him and had awaited their arrival.

They had finally reached their living quarters, and Ruben opened the tiny door with a clanging, a screeching and a thud, releasing a mixture of strange and foul-smelling odours which scraped Lafty's throat and made his eyes water. A quick scan of this long, oblong-shaped cabin made him more depressed than when he had left his home. Everything was painted in black or grey, giving the place a dull and dark feel, and evoking a feeling that he had entered an endless cave. There were rows and rows of beds lining both sides, with small spaces between in which the sailors could store their belongings. Lafty wished his father could understand his predicament. Tears trickled down his worried face and his wandering thoughts filled his head with haunting questions. What is this place? he asked himself. Is it hell or just a prison? Could it get worse? But there was little time for him to dwell on these thoughts. Ruben was in high spirits, his plans were taking shape and he was about to put the finishing touch to them.

'This is where you'll stay', said Ruben, 'and this is your bed. I don't suppose you have ever seen beds like these. You will be sleeping on the top and I'll sleep at the bottom. They are called bunks', he explained. Lafty listened but said nothing. In fact he had not spoken a word throughout their travels. 'We'll both share this space.'

Lafty smiled and sat on the bed, which was about the same size as the one on which he had slept at home. The covering had a dark and rustic look that seemed strange. At first glance it could be mistaken for a blanket, but he hadn't seen a blanket made from that kind of material before. Quietly he waited for his father to tell him more about his rich aunt, but the choking, musty smells got stronger with every breath, leaving him puzzled at his new environment.

Ruben's main priority was to get Lafty settled quickly, so that he could make the start time for his working shift which was fast approaching. He wanted the lad to feel comfortable before he went, but the strangeness of the cabin gave off an intimidating air, not the right sort of environment for a frightened boy. And yet Ruben did not give much thought to his son's feelings. As a sailor he had become accustomed to the dark, musty smells and cramped conditions. So he was not too concerned even though the poor boy's eyes were watering. He sat beside Lafty, and for some reason he did something strange and unexpected. Maybe he was pricked by his conscience. In an attempt to offer some reassurance, he gently wrapped his giant muscles around Lafty and made him feel safe. In doing so, Ruben's bulging muscles suddenly took the shape of a mountain top, lifting the boy's spirit, making his eyes sparkle. His face came alive and his brilliant white teeth shone in the darkness. This was the kind of bonding for which he had been searching. His inquisitive mind went into overdrive. He wanted to say something like, 'What strong muscles you have, Dad. When I grow up I hope my muscles will be like yours.' He held onto his father's muscles as though he would never see them again. His fingers, sliding over the rippling contours, seemed to speak without sound and somehow Ruben understood what they were trying to say.

He replied, 'They will. They will one day, son. But first we must talk. There are rules aboard this ship that you must obey, so let me enlighten you as to what they are. First, I will show you the wash-place and toilets, and then I will explain what you must and must not do. No running down the alleyways, no whistling on board, no loitering in the canteen, no smoking below and no hanging from the mast after dark.'

Ruben talked for nearly an hour, which left Lafty to wonder whether his father was going mad or the happiness of holding him had gone to his head. Lafty was about to ask what clothes he should change into, not that he had many, when Ruben said in strong voice, 'And never go naked when I'm not here.' It was too much for little Lafty to take in, so he rolled over onto the bed and went to sleep.

'One more thing Lafty,' Ruben went on. 'There are four of us mates in our gang and we'll all take turns in caring for you. They are Mud, Scruffy, Dusty and me. We each work opposite shifts so one of us will always be here.' By then the little boy had become so tired that he had fallen into a deep sleep and did not clearly hear the names.

CHAPTER 4

Untold Plans

Ruben was late to relieve Mud and so was forced to leave Lafty asleep in the cabin. He had hoped Scruffy and Dusty would have turned up by then; he wanted to remind them of his plans and their agreement to help. It was also his intention to tell them of the role Lafty would play. Having been given the reputation of Mr Charmer, the ladies man with a wife in every port, he knew that Mud would want to know if he had managed to reaffirm his conquest and nothing less than an affirmative would do for an answer. Ruben, being what he was, knew that his reputation should be maintained at all cost. Telling the truth was not an option. He had to plot a story that would be convincing to Mud. But whether it was a result of the foul smells or the excitement of his son being aboard, memories of his conquest went clear from his head. Only the safety of his son Lafty was of any concern. In his hurry, thoughts of his past began to dance through his head. He had to make changes and temper his lavish lifestyle if only for the boy's sake, he thought. With the ship calling at three ports, the journey could take a few days, including shore leave. This could be a short spell so he would reject going ashore, which he knew would not please his mates. It might dent his reputation, but that was the chance he had to take. Making his way, he called to see Scruffy and Dusty, but they were not at their work stations. They had disappeared into some corner. Still, he continued the search for his mates, optimistic of his ambitious plan. Selfish though it was, the reward would be good. No one actually knew what his plans were, so close was he keeping them to his chest, but to make good those plans a final adjustment had to be made before Lafty arrived at his destination. Ruben was stumped. He had to get a message to his sister and warn her of Lafty's arrival. Perhaps a telegram at his next port of call, he thought. He had to be careful, though, about Mud becoming wise to his plans before they were perfected. Mud knew Ruben's style better then any other, so he was hiding his plans from Mud. Mud also knew about Ruben's financial difficulties, that Ruben could not leave the ship when she docked in some of the ports they visited in fear of those he had tricked.

Ruben was a sporty person who attracted more friends then any other of his mates. Not that they were jealous of him. On the contrary, they thought he was trying to be too clever and dreaded the day when his actions caught up with him. Ruben believed that life was for living and everyone should take advantage of every moment they had. His outlook seemed logical, but skirted round the responsibility he had to others, especially his children. By his actions it appeared he was doing those children a favour by accepting them as such. Neither Mud Scruffy nor Dusty liked Ruben's lifestyle, but they were mates and had sailed together on the same ship all their working lives. It was too late for him to change. Moreover he was not an evil man. His presence electrified his surroundings and he was always in demand, though mainly by ladies who were particularly interested in his physique and his incurable wit and charm, a charm that never failed to weave a web of attraction around those he met.

Ruben also had a grave weakness. His charming approach, razor sharp wit and tricky attitudes had a habit of letting him down and inflaming tempers, resulting in scuffles. Ironically, Ruben could not adequately defend himself against those of murderous intent, whose delight was in brute force. Physically, he was a very strong person; though there was a gentle side to him. This hulk of a man could not inflict bodily harm on anyone. Though his appearance gave the perception he was a tough guy, in reality Ruben was as soft as a kitten and gentle as a lamb. Whether or not he was afraid of scarring the physique he adored was never tested. One thing was proven; his attractive physical appearance was a magnet.

Nevertheless, his friends were the opposite. They loved a good scrap and some seedy rum bar or another was the ideal place to find it on their nights out. While Ruben's slippery tongue and tricky attitudes provoked the challenge they needed, his mates would obligingly take the fight to conmen or women while he gently slipped away. Mind you, these people were no more then parasites that made their homes and livelihood in these establishments. Their aim was to make a quick buck without caring who they hurt in the process. They were rough-looking people, whose dress code betrayed their identities to frequent visitors such as sailors. They were lawless individuals operating in a lawless environment. Their language and tricks knew no bounds; maiming and killing was part of their day-to-lives. They were people who had accepted death or injury at an instant. It did not matter how or when these acts occurred; it was more important how rich or how clever they were.

Ruben was a smart dresser whose bulging muscles and charming sense of humour made him the centre of attention, and his arrival would sometimes be seen as a threat and spark a challenge to these cut-throat operators. He was also a fast learner who indulged in the kind of trickery that gave him the zest to nurture his charms. Having visited many sea ports, he had picked up and developed new ideas that gave him numerous opportunities to test his wits at exploiting those less knowledgeable than him and thereby boost his overrated confidence. But the ladies would be first to seize upon his repartee, convinced he was a man of learning, and that riches weren't far away. Many of these could not read or write and were unable to understand the meanings of the words he spoke. His words sounded grand in the presence of others, making him appear intelligent and respectable enough to win their hearts. His dilemma usually came when rivalry broke out among the gathering ladies, resulting in fights to lay claim on his armour. A battle line would be drawn and men with something to prove would line up to join an extended fight, while the lucky lady or ladies would shout to Ruben, 'Come with me and I'll make your armour safe.' Those were great moments for Ruben. It was times such as those when he lived his dreams.

Young and fit, with no care in the world, a wizard at the card table who managed to win all his games, he was a big-headed person. It was his three friends who made him that way. They backed him in everything he did, collaborating in his conspiracies to make him win and look good. Then, at the end of their rampaging night of games, they would fight; split their winnings and walk away smiling.

These sessions boosted his position, leaving others with the feeling that he was untouchable, unstoppable; too clever to get caught. But Ruben wasn't as infallible as he thought. The passing years were taking their toll. He was becoming complacent, and his clever trickery was beginning to fail. He could no longer visit the seedy bars as often as he would have liked. And, one by one, the ladies became wise to the slippery acts of a fraudster.

And while he slipped from grace, deserted by the loose women, an alarming weakness surfaced. Ruben loved young and beautiful virgins – but it was a game he played that was threatening the friendship of his mates. The man could not help himself; he was as slick as the smoothly flowing ink of a ballpoint pen. Inviting his friends' daughters to his bed was not the right thing to do and he was on the verge of being ostracised by them if he did not change.

Ruben thought of the good times he had with his friends. He could not tell them of a plan he had yet to finalise but still he tried desperately to figure out a way to divulge it to them. Reality began to rattle his brain. They were all getting older, he thought, their heyday was almost behind them, and he could not take Lafty to his home. So why was he taking him to meet the sister with whom he hardly ever spoke? There were so many unanswered questions, not even he knew the answers. Mud had been Ruben's closest friend, closer than any of his brothers or sisters. Yet Ruben's secretive attitudes had created doubt and he stood to lose the trust of his best friend. They had fought many battles and won many games, tricked many people as they had travelled, but they had always kept each other's secrets wherever they went.

When Ruben finally reached his workstation his heartbeat echoed the hooves of horses on a sandy tract. What could he do to make this burden lighter? Sooner or later they will all know my plans, he told himself, but for now this little secret remains with me. Their friendships were physical and tactile in nature. Greeting each other meant touching, pushing and shoving. It was a bonding ritual that rekindled and cemented the happiness that flowed between friends. Their eyes would light up, their brilliant white teeth would sparkle and set their smiling faces aglow, and there were hand gestures and body language to match. Mud was glad to see Ruben because he thought Ruben was late getting aboard. So while Mud worked and waited, he had no idea that Ruben was settling Lafty, and by then he was tired and did not want to talk. All he wanted was to hand over the watch and get to sleep. He was relieved at Ruben's arrival. Better late than never, he thought. At last he could have that well deserved rest. But Ruben had other things on his mind and was in one of his usual buoyant moods, explaining that Lafty was on board, and was a sleep in the cabin. He was rattling away ten to the dozen reminding Mud of the promise they had made sometime ago about looking after Lafty, which wasn't what Mud's tired brain wanted to hear. They would have shook hands on the agreement, a commitment neither one would break. Mud was in shock, as thoughts of horror gripped his head. Why had he agreed to help with a plan that he didn't know enough about? He became nervous with sickly feelings rumbling through his stomach, and heard a voice saying, 'change your mind'. But, it was too late, and emptiness filled his soul. 'What could I have done differently?' he wondered. 'After all, there are no secrets between us'. Still, Mud waited patiently to hear Ruben's explanation of his plans. But Ruben talked instead about meeting Lafty's mother and the good times they had had; nothing of his plans or why Lafty was aboard.

With deep hesitation Mud began to doubt their friendship, wondering whether he had done something that could have caused Ruben to lose favour in his confidence, toss their friendship into turmoil. His brain searched his past for clues as to where he could have gone wrong. Their friendship had begun from childhood, and even though everyone called him Mud, his real name was Don. He inherited the name Mud at the age of seven. It was his first day at school and like most kids he was a shy, nervous boy, even among his friends. He was worse still among strangers. Heavy rain had fallen earlier that day and flooded the schoolyard. So, most children had to wade through the thick muddy water to get home, which was great fun at first. But things got frightening when one of the bullies thought it would be funny to splash dirty water, making a mess of his clean clothes. It was very demoralising in front of other children and to make matters worse they laughed uncontrollably at Don's demise. School was a very disappointing exercise; he was furious and helpless. He was too small and too weak to stand up to those boys. Looking at his clothes he was scared to face his mother, who might not believe that someone else had muddied them, his only school clothes. It would be unlikely that he would be able to wear them the following day. Even if his mother was to wash them that night, they would never dry in time to wear the following morning. He was also sure to get a hiding from my father with his belt.

All four schoolboys were in the same class at school. Don was not the only one fuming at the bully-boys' tactic; he had three friends, Scruffy, Dusty and Ruben, who were as upset and wanted to do something that would dirty the bully-boys' clothes. There were others, too, who were urging Don to fight for his rights no matter how big the boys were. Don was afraid but he was overwhelmed by the emotional shouts and screams. It also made the big boys feel cocky and they pushed harder until he fell over. This time Don fell face-first into the muddy water and emerged a terrible mess. The shouting turned the fight into an all-out action as the four boys jumped the bully-boys, thumping, kicking, biting and stoning them with the muddy soil. To Don's relief a teacher saw the fighting mob and broke it up, but by the time the fight was over Don had had the biggest hiding of his life. Those bully-boys knew how to fight and were too big and strong for Don and his friends. The fight left him in an awful state. His clothes were so dirty you could not tell what colour they were. It would take his mother at lease two days to rid them of the muddy stains. And, from that day on, Don was called Mud and the name stuck fast.

And yet before that dreaded day, Don was a very quiet boy who loved to read and make toy boats. And the closeness of the river gave an open invitation for all four boys to spend many hours playing sailor with those paper boats, taking turns to be the captain. Don was not the brightest of boys, but he grew up able to read and write well enough to get a job he now had as a sailor. Both he and the ship were ageing at the same speed. Lots of history had passed between those mates since childhood, but they remained the closest of friends.

Although Mud had not met Lafty he knew a great deal about him through Ruben. With Ruben's marital affair thrust on them after so many years, it set off an uneasy feeling that caused him to reflect on the antics of their past. He could take comfort that at no time had a child ever been involved in any of their schemes. His brain was in frenzy, and could not think straight. Ruben told him that his son Lafty was part of a plan, which he knew nothing about and was of great concern. Mud could take comfort from his knowledge of his friend and be reassured, that he know that Ruben would not harm a child, let alone his own son. But what if someone got hurt during the process of carrying out his plans? What then, he thought, and who could he blame?

Leaning over the deck railings watching the swell of the mighty sea as its roaring waves slashed against the ship hull, occasionally leaving the deck awash, he could only wonder what he would do if one day his misdeeds should catch up with him. There were many unanswered questions stemming from his adventures across the Islands. How many children had he fathered? If the truth was known, the result could be shocking. This was not a good idea, he heard himself say. He had to know what Ruben plans were.

Mud turned to Ruben and was about to ask the question when, as if by magic, Ruben stopped him in his tracks and said, 'Mud, I have something to tell you, but it will have to wait for another day.'

'Good news I hope', Mud replied.

'Wait and see', said Ruben.

Mud felt relieved. At last the man had spoken. Maybe it was not as bad as he had led himself to believe after all. In cheerful mood and with a smile on his face he set off to see this new sailor, Lafty, whose presence had created quite a stir. He slid down the steps like a fireman on a greasy pole and hurried to the cabin wondering what he would find.

Although they were of one gang, Mud did not share his secrets with the other two, Dusty and Scruffy. But halfway along the narrow, dingy gangway, he met Dusty, crouched like a bundle of waste rags. He was painting the dull rusting walls where the paint had flaked, exposing cracks.

'The seawater is to blame', he grumbled.

More like the age of the ship, thought Mud. If the seawater should pour through it would be our fault that we chose to be here. Mud stopped and stood over his friend, brandishing a smile. Startled by his presence, Dusty looked more worried than surprised. Mud said, 'Dusty I am on my way to see our new visitor. I was told he is resting in the cabin.'

Dusty turned to him. 'Who would that be?'

'It's Ruben's son Lafty,' said Mud. 'He's sleeping in the cabin as we speak.' His rustic voice lowered to a whisper. 'We've been landed with another of Ruben's bright ideas. Do you remember the promise we suppose to have made when he first told us that his boy would join him on his return journey?'

'Yes I remember.'

'Well, the boy is here and we are obliged to help in his care, so we will have to share the burden between us.'

Dusty burst out laughing, not the kind of reaction Mud was expecting. It was not clear to Dusty that his friend Mud was not playing a joke on him. After all, this was something they regularly did to each other. He rose to his feet. 'Well, if that's my promise then I'd better carry it out to the best of my ability.'

'So had I,' Mud replied. 'But I thought Ruben was in one of his funny moods when he made the suggestion. I'd also forgotten all about it.'

'What do I know about taking care of a child, especially on the high seas? The man is mad,' said Dusty.

'How right you are, Dusty, but a promise is a promise. More than that, a child is involved. We will have to do our best for him.'

'Have you seen the boy, Mud?'

'Not yet. Ruben has only just relieved me from my shift and I am on my way to see this son he has been talking about.'

Dusty crouched position had left him with uncomfortable feelings in his legs. With a paint-brush in one hand, and a piece of multicoloured cloth in the other, he tried to straighten his over-worked body that seemed to be covered in more paint than the walls. His body was nervously shaking and his eyes seemed glazed. The rolling motions of a sailing ship did not help either. Neither of the men could take in the seriousness of their promise.

'A cargo ship is not the right place for a boy with no experience of sailing,' said Dusty. 'It's too rough, too dirty, and much too dangerous for a lad who has never sailed on a ship of this size. All I can say, Mud, is it was rum talk. We were all at the rum bar and weren't thinking straight when we agreed. It appears we made a mistake.'

'I couldn't believe he would carry out this foolish thing,' said Mud.

Dusty leaned against the freshly painted wall to steady his weakened body. It was either that or fall on his face. His sea legs had gone and he was losing control. Mud quickly held him and got him steady, but there was something about Dusty's movement that was more surprising to Mud. Dusty was a hardened sailor, so why were his legs so weak? Could he have been drinking? Whether or not he had been drinking, Ruben had a lot to answer to, they both decided.

Dusty had another two hours before he ended his shift and he could not walk away from his job even to take a short break. The bosun was a strict man. His motto was each man was given a job that must be completed at the end of that day; anything less and he would regret ever having set foot on that bosun's ship. Mud was on pin and needles. He wanted to go and see to Lafty, but he had to stay and make sure Dusty was safe. He could not understand why Dusty was so fragile. What could have caused the sudden change? Mud could not hang around much longer but he was worried that Dusty might collapse. Maybe there was something more that Mud should know? Dusty's behaviour made things looked more twisted than Mud first thought. Anyway few deep breaths of the foul damp air and Dusty seem ready to resume his task.

'Are you able to carry on Dusty?' Mud asked.

'I'm okay now,' he replied. 'It must have been the paint fumes, and the rum I had last night.'

Who's he trying to kid? Mud thought. However, he could be right on one thing, when they had said yes to Ruben they had thought he was pulling their legs. Ruben was supposed to love his son very much and yet he had exposed him to a dangerous voyage aboard a ship that was no better than a rusting bucket, where disaster could happen in a flash. But there was nothing they could do at that late stage. Neither one had the answer, though they knew that none of their children would ever sail on that ship.

Mud walked away, burdened by Ruben's plans. Dusty had resumed painting in a crouching position, picking up from where he left off, trying to block Ruben's plans from his head. But his thoughts were on a collision course and there was no easy solution. Soon his search for an answer led him to one of his mother's sayings. She always used to say, 'Every negative act usually breeds a positive reaction.' So, maybe something good might come from Ruben's plans. Regardless how bad things might seem, they were shipmates, brothers in arms. It was a case of one for all and all for one, like the musketeers. Their friendship compelled him to do whatever it took to make Lafty comfortable. Furthermore, it was imperative that they did everything they could to keep their friendship intact. Dusty was not a handsome man, nor was he a clever person, though he played an important role within the gang. His rough, raggedy appearance was deceiving, and his friend described him as the sheep that followed; the dependable one who was always willing to help. Someone they could trust. Dusty would follow his mates to the end and, if need be, die for them. He was a dedicated friend, and as hard as nails, both of which were qualities a seafarer needed.

Dusty was also an only child. By the time he was born his parents had already reached middle age. Dusty was the child they thought they could never have. With joy in their hearts and love in their souls they gave Dusty protection, affection, and everything else that they could give. He was smothered by over-caring parents. Their protective attitude was somewhat different to many other parents. Not only did they shroud him from as many knocks as he grew up; they also prepared him to survive in a rough and tough world. Rightly or wrongly, his parents taught him every skill they knew, or could think of, which would give him a head start over many of his friends. More than any of this gang of four, he could carry out any domestic chores with both eyes closed. Dusty's parents had equipped him for any eventuality. He was so domesticated that he hated dirt and so was always busy cleaning. If something needed cleaning, Dusty would be the first to find a brush and sweep away the mess. Neither he nor his partner had children, even though he loved her and they had lived together for twenty years. They had intended to marry, but he had not wanted to hurry her, preferring instead to wait until she felt she was ready. But while they waited their biological clock had been ticking, and, fortunately or unfortunately, he escaped the responsibility of fathering a child.

Though friendship was vital to the gang Dusty was not faultless. He liked a drink of rum, and when he drank the stuff his fear would disappear. He was not choosy about which particular brand of drink, either, even methylated spirits. Dusty was like no other. But, surprisingly, he held the deep principles of a disciplined person, was as gentle as a lamb, and was an angel who would not even use swearwords onboard ship. Dusty was talented, a jack of all trades who could do virtually anything that was asked of him. He could be joker, a clown and a comedian, or a man who inspired with every breath he took. He was so good at so many things, and that made him the idea minder for Lafty. Blessed with a magnificent pair of lungs, every time he sang the melody set everyone's soul alive, though it was a pity he could not enjoy singing without a drink inside him. But, best of all, he had the will power to control his love for the firewater, something which was greatly admired. He never drank while he was working. Drinking was for enjoyment. That, to him, was his greatest asset.

A lovable shipmate, he soon became the ship's dog's body who never frowned or grumbled. He was always smiling, which amazed the others. Only Ruben knew the real Dusty. It could be said that

Ruben was onto a good thing by having Dusty's friendship; even Mud shared those views, though he did not understand what it was that created the defining bond between them. Mud was sure that Dusty was their dream ticket to Lafty's happiness, and Lafty would love Dusty's smiling face.

Dusty regained his composure. His trembling knees stopped. Great, thought Mud. There's still a lot of fight in the old sea dog. The violent sea had gradually become calm, as if the fire that had been burning inside had suddenly gone out. It was time that Mud saw Lafty. He had become concerned that Lafty had been left for far too long alone in that dark, smelly den with no one to talk to and nowhere to go. He was probably frightened out of his mind by now, Mud thought, and wondering what his Father had gone and done. Mud hurried away from Dusty, trying to get to Lafty as fast as he could, but he was not getting there fast. Ruben's mysterious plans seemed to have sent him into a dream. The burden of not knowing what was happening had made him nervousness.

It was fair to say that children of Lafty's age regularly worked on the ship as cabin boys. Their supple bodies made it easy to slip swiftly in and out of tiny doorways, narrow gangways and the sort of cramped conditions that were sometimes difficult for grown men. Their nimble hands and feet were ideally suited to operate in these places. But they were rough characters who would kill for a penny; not the sort of people to care for a defenceless boy. While Mud contemplated the seriousness of Ruben's actions anger filled his head. It was reasonable to think that Mud was upset because he had a son the same age as Lafty. The balance as he saw it was not in Lafty's favour. And Mud was afraid that Ruben might turn Lafty into another cabin boy, which he was determined would not happen. Lafty was an innocent passenger, and should be treated as such, he thought. They had been friends all their lives, thought Mud, surely Ruben would listen to him? Mud had decided to take a stand and persuade his friend to consider the value of their friendship.

CHAPTER 5

The Ship

The ship was their lifeline for trade between the islands and had been making the same voyage year in, year out. Lafty's destination was a three-day journey; a journey propelled by his father with many obstacles to be overcome, and many lessons to be learned. Hopefully, his youth and innocence would help him to quickly understand his father's lifestyle as a sailor. It would also perhaps equip his young brain with experiences that many grown-ups would probably envy.

Mud had by now reached the tiny door that was rarely left open. Surprised to find it ajar, he pushed upon it until it clanged against the wooden bunk bed. And there was Lafty, curled up like a discarded bundle. A newborn lamb in a barn filled with straw, a pitiful sight to behold. Mud had failed to notice if the boy was awake, and mumbled something like, 'Are you asleep?' But the frightened boy did not move in case Mud was a cutthroat. All kinds of weird thoughts thundered through his mind. As a child he had heard many stories of men who ate boys for breakfast, and with Mud stood over him, and not knowing what he would do, his heartbeat quickened like a galloping hyena. He was terrified as to what might happen next. The thought that he had reached the end of his life did enter his head.

'Where is my father?' he cried, but the sound did not come out. Memories of his mother's tearful cries while she talked to his father had raised his suspicions. She must have known then that I was going to be eaten, he told himself. How could she do this to me after she told me that she loved me? Was she lying to me? That would explain why she kissed me so many times and did not want to let go of my hands. If this is what my mother wanted then, so be it, but if I should live, I could never love her again. His face was awash with tears, and like the penetrating sound of the jungle drum his heart beat inside his chest and left his body numb. In silence Lafty waited for what he believed was his bitter end. He did not know that Mud was a gentle person with only love in his heart. He was becoming more and more terrified as the forceful energy of Mud's presence bore down on him.

Mud, too, was confused. He did not know what to do next, so he did the only thing he could, which was gain the boy's attention. He gently touched Lafty, though Lafty thought he was about to die and became hysterical. He leapt from his straw bundle, screaming as loudly as he could and bolted through the tiny door like a bullet down the gangway. Mud quickly followed and caught up with him at the end of the gangway, shaking like a wet kitten. The disabled boy's hands were flapping faster than the wings of a pigeon as he tried to find the words to say, 'Don't eat me sir, I'm a good boy and I'll never cry again.'

Lafty's sorrowful face broke Mud's heart, even though Mud did not know what the boy was trying to say. What have I done? wondered Mud. But with a loving smile and gentle, caring touch he brought calm to Lafty's troubled mind. Filled with love, care and compassion, Mud held Lafty as he would have held his own son, and hurriedly took the boy back to their cabin before the bosun or anyone else arrived. That was too close for comfort, Mud thought. He hoped there would never be a repeat performance or they could all lose their jobs. By the time they got to the cabin, Lafty had become calm. Whatever Mud had told him, it must have worked.

The trauma of the day was bearing heavily on their minds, but what else could they do than sit in silence and survey each other?

Lafty did not realise that not everyone could understand him like his mother. She knew his needs and could relate to his gestures. So he tried to ask Mud who he was. Although there were no spoken words, Mud had somehow surmised what the boy wanted to know and quickly said, 'I am your father's friend. Did he not tell you about me, or mention my name? They call me Mud. However, if you're going to be my friend, my real name is Don.'

Lafty smiled and with an outstretched arm he shook Don's hand. What he really wanted to say was, 'No, sir, my father forgot to tell me the names of his friends; nor can I remember hearing your name.' Lafty then handed Mud the piece of paper that the man at the desk had stamped. Mud took the note and read it. It said, 'His name is Lafty and he is going to see his aunt whom he hasn't met. He's been told she's a very nice lady and she lives on a beautiful island.'

Mud's face radiated with a smile that reassured Lafty of his reply. 'I bet she is nice,' he said. It was very uncomfortable for Mud. Lafty had yet to speak a word and that left him in a dilemma. He began to blame himself for Lafty's failure to speak. It's my fault, he thought. I have frightened the boy and as a result, he has lost his speech.

With Ruben's plans on his mind, his thoughts wandered. There was more to it than met the eye, he thought. 'Do you know the name of the island where your Aunt lives?' Mud asked.

But Lafty's twisted face, bulging eyes and opening mouth could not confirm Mud's suspicions. Lafty wanted to say, 'My father did not tell me the name of this island, but my mother said my aunt lived in a great big house near to the sea.'

Once again Mud could work out the answers mainly by Lafty's frantic hand gestures and body movements. 'That's sounds wonderful,' he said. 'I wouldn't mind living in a place like that.'

In a bid to bring comfort to the distressed boy, Ruben had told Lafty all about the place he was going to live during their journey to the ship. He told Lafty of the many varieties of fruit the island produced, and the choices he would have, such as apple, mango, pear, banana, sweet-sap, sour-sap, orange and guava, star apple, custard apple, melons and lots, lots more. Fruits were in season all the year round on this island and he could never get hungry with so many nice things to eat. He would not be bored, either, because there were plenty of friendly children with many places to go and lots to see and love. It could be a magical place, Ruben had told him. In silence, Lafty body rose and fell with his beating heart and breathing lungs, and Mud was left to think of what his friend would say.

'I bet he told you a lot of nice things; how happy you will be.'
The boy nodded his head.

I bet he did, Mud thought. That rotten dog. 'Are you hungry, Lafty? After all you've been aboard a long time.'

Lafty shook his head to say, 'No sir.' His mother had given him bread, which he had not eaten, but he would like a drink. His hands made the signs that Mud could understand. Once again Lafty's skills in gesturing helped him to obtain what he wanted.

Mud got up, walked over to the place where they stored their personal belongings, and took out an old enamel mug. It had so many chips it looked like a Dalmatian dog. He had never seen a mug with so many chips; some were so bad that the rusted steel showed through. But that was Mud's mug and no one, least of all Mud, cared. Lafty mother's was poor, and could hardly afford to feed her family without leftovers from the master's table, and had used her calabash container to take home the food, without worrying about it leaking out. If her calabash container was not available, she would use banana or the cocoa leaves. Failing that she would use the oldest container she could find in her master's house, but nothing was as awful as Mud's enamel mug. Mud slipped through the door as fast as a flash and returned with a full mug of water to quench Lafty's thirst. At sea and with nowhere else to go, he could not refuse to drink from that mug, so he drank the water and was happy.

That was Lafty's second lesson on the open seas, Mud thought. Lafty then took a good look at the mattress, which he could not have seen properly when he first entered the cabin. He had been too nervous, too upset and too tired to consider his surroundings carefully: the dark, painted walls, narrow gangway and the foul smells of grease, soot and body odour. If you are a sailor, you have to be tough, he remembered. But he had not realised it would be that bad. He looked at the bed. The grass-filled sugar bag mattress and pillow were rough and smelly, and overrun with flees. If the flees failed to get him, the sharp-ended straw and the other creepy crawlies would be delighted to finish off the job.

In the short time he had slept, his body had caught fire. He scratched and scratched until his skin began to peel. It was a shattering experience that marred his boyhood dreams. If this is what sea life is about, it's not the life for me, he thought. But where is the adventure my mother was so excited about?

Lafty could not think straight; he was confused. What his mother had told him about his father did not match the environment he was experiencing. They were completely different. The water tasted the same as it did at home, though maybe a bit woody from the barrels that kept it fresh. But the flaked enamel mug made no difference. His pleasing eyes expressed a vote of thanks. With a quenched thirst and a relaxed mind, he attempted to embrace what was his home for however long his father decided.

The sun had waved goodbye to a cloudless sky and invited the moon to smile, but Mud was still concerned for Lafty's safety. This is going to be a long night, he thought, and began to think of things that could make the boy happy. Ruben's shift would not end until the following morning; a long time to wait should the boy stay awake. He felt pretty sure Lafty was no longer thirsty, but was he hungry? Lafty had given Mud the impression he had eaten bread and was full. Even with all that assurance Mud was not totally satisfied; there was a grave sadness in the boy's eyes that made him feel uneasy.

'So, what else can I do to make you comfortable, lad?'

Lafty wasn't responding to what Mud was trying to say, and there was little more Mud could do. Should I tell him a story? Mud wondered. Yes, that's what I'll do. But first I must wash and changed these clothes.

'Stay here Lafty, I won't be long,' he said, and went to wash the black, greasy coal dust stains from his face, hands and feet. Mud maintained the engine, which was the dirtiest place aboard the ship. He had to keep the boilers fully charged and the giant drive-shaft properly greased. However, looking at the state of his clothes, hands and face you could be forgiven for thinking that Mud had more grease and coal on him than the engine did. At the end of his working shifts he became a frightening sight in a darkened cabin.

While Mud washed, the giant swells of the mighty sea tossed the ship violently, and made Lafty's stomach queasy. The water he had drunk earlier began to bubble in his throat like a runaway train, and churned his stomach like an active volcano. He felt light-headed, and his eyelids kept closing as though he wanted nothing better than to sleep. Suddenly his mouth flew open and a bucketful of sick covered the mattress. The little boy was shocked more than he had ever been in his life and once again became hysterical. He cried for his mother even though she was nowhere in sight. He began to wonder what she had done to him, and began to blame her for the way he felt. In the meantime the watery liquid quickly drained through the porous filling of the mattress. There was nothing Lafty could do other than sit and wait for Mud to return, though it seemed he'd been away forever. His heart was pounding; his nervous knees trembled and his fragile body was weakened by his disturbed mind. Worried what Mud might do or say when he returned, he began to conjure up all sorts of weird thoughts.

In the distance Mud could hear a commotion and became frightened. 'Holy God', he said, 'something has happened to Lafty.' He ran as fast as he could, breaking the all ship's rules. Frightened out of his mind he arrived in the cabin half dressed and half washed, with black soapy water dripping from his face and flowing like a stream along the floor behind him. He arrived to find Lafty awash with tears. Puffing like an overloaded train he repeatedly asked Lafty, 'What's wrong, what's wrong?' but the boy did not speak. Mud looked for signs of injury but there were none visible. Repeatedly he asked the boy where it hurt, and still no answer. It was clear to Mud that Lafty was in shock, but why? Lafty's fright had created feelings of guilt that were clouding his mind. After all he had not long given Lafty a mug of water, which he had drunk, and he had been settled when he left. So what could make him shake like a drowning kitten? I have done it again, he thought. To have caused one scare is bad enough but two, in a short time, that is not good. How will I explain this to Ruben? Unable to pinpoint the boy's pain, his brain surged with questions and his thoughts became a raging fire. If anything should happen to Lafty, it would be easier to jump overboard than face Ruben's wrath.

With sadness in his eyes he looked at the boy and mumbled, 'I haven't got an answer to your cries. All I can do is to sit beside and comfort you.' Mud gently whispered in the little boy's ears saying, 'Hush now, there is no need to feel afraid, no one is going to hurt you as long as I am here.'

Mud's comforting words were an assuring tonic that brought peace to the little boy's troubled mind. In relief Lafty inhaled a deep breath, and with it the foul smelling discharge and choking, dusty, dungeon cabin, and somehow accepted that Mud was a good person. Mud was used to all the ship's smells but there was a new smell he could not detect; something was not right, he thought. It was only then, when he saw the result of Lafty's mishap on the floor that he became aware of what had happened.

'So this is what it's all about, hah, me lad? Don't you worry now, we are shipmates, and shipmates look out for each other. You won't be left alone again, I promise. And tomorrow you'll meet new friends and they, my lad, are the best. They will make you feel better. You might even forget all about today.'

The partly-washed Mud sat with Lafty, nurturing thoughts that the boy was settling down. He knew that he did not smell great, although he was not as dirty as he had been earlier, and did not dismiss the idea of finishing his wash as soon as it was safe to do so. His strong arms, gentle touch and kinds words began to build a bridge of friendship.

Mud was busy talking, with no thought that the boy was not listening, nor that the violent ship was playing havoc with Lafty's rumbling gut and he was choked with fear, fear that his time had come and he was going to die, and that his mother was not there. And to make matters worse, his stomach was at odds with his brain, sending messages he was powerless to stop. One message said, 'Open your mouth and let me out or I'll burst your belly button.' In reply, the other one said, 'Be still and everything will be okay.' Lafty fought to stay still, but the pressure was too great for a frightened boy; he had to concede and take what seemed a very serious warning. He opened his mouth as wide as it could and made a painful growl. And in the flash of an eye, and like a fireman's hose, he ejected an almighty spray all over Mud's half washed, half dressed body.

Mud became angry, an immediate reaction to a frightening situation, but quickly transferred that energy to Ruben's shameful demise. Ruben's selfish plans had placed his son in a position that made it easy for anyone to take a dim view of the boy's crying. His evoked conscience forced him to withhold his anger but thought that Ruben should have been the one here dealing with the hassle. Lafty was Ruben's son and whatever Ruben's plans were, they were his plans and his responsibility. Ruben seemed to know what the effect of his plans would be on his friends, when he seconded them to care for his son. After all, they were his only friends. He knew them inside out, and could rely on them. Ruben also knew they could handle any embarrassment, even the worries of a child they had never met. I suppose there was no one else he could have asked, Mud told himself.

But Ruben should have thought more of his son and realised that he had never been on board a ship or sailed the sea. Mud was both furious and surprised at Ruben's actions, and could not understand why the boy was not properly prepared for journey that left him at the mercy of the mighty swells, foul smells, an intimidating environment, and a violent ship that could overbalance the strongest sailor let alone a small boy. Those thoughts made Mud fearsomely resolute to see that Ruben paid for his selfishness one way or another.

Curled up like a bundle of rags, and sobbing for his mother's attention, Lafty was showing signs of being deeply distressed. He was not responding as Mud had expected. So Mud began to look beyond the boy's feeble expression and became suspicious of his mother Marybell's actions. It seemed to him that Marybell did not know Ruben as well as she might have thought. What was she thinking, he wondered, when she allowed Ruben to take her son away at such a young age to travel the sea, with no knowledge of its dangers. Even though boys of Lafty's age were at sea, they probably came from families of seafarers, or they lived around the sea, and were aware of the dangers that it posed. That was not the case with Lafty; he had been born deep in the countryside, and only moved close to the sea when his mother's obsession to find Ruben became acute. More than likely he might not have seen or sailed the sea; it was too sudden to launch a boy of his experience into an environment as hostile as the sea. That had not been the right thing to do. Mud's emotions were clearly disturbed, but no matter what his thoughts were, they could not change the actions that had already been taken. Neither could they change Lafty's feelings.

Mucus and tears flowed effortlessly down Lafty's face, and Mud's gentle, sympathetic strokes brought relief to the saddened mind of a distraught boy. Soon the erratic breathing and thumping heartbeat steadied. Mud held the boy close to his body. His fatherly care was reaching out to Lafty; he felt good and for a moment neither the dingy lighting nor the foul smells mattered. Partially wet, he carefully lifted the end of his shirt and dried Lafty's waterlogged face. Although a raging anger burned within his soul, he had to take a rational approach to what could become an explosive situation. It was vital that Mud did not allow his feelings to alert the frightened boy. That would be the last thing Mud wanted to happen. As Lafty's irregular breathing calmed, so Mud's anger began to subside, exposing cracks of rational thinking, and one by one Mud eliminated the negative aspects of Ruben's persona.

Reflecting on their friendship, trying to appreciate Ruben's character, the things they had done together, and the places they had been, soon rekindled feelings of fulfilment that left him in no doubt. Ruben would not do anything that could remotely bring harm to a child, especially his own son. Mud could not bring his thoughts to think of anything other than to the good of that child. Though he was sceptical of Ruben's plan, he believed it could be of long term benefit to Lafty and his sister. He also took comfort from the fact Ruben was from a large family, some of whom were very rich people and could provide a better lifestyle for Lafty than Ruben or Lafty's mother. With those facts in mind, Mud decided he should not pre-judge the result of Ruben's mysterious plan.

Mud was not on his own in thinking in this way. For many years Lafty's mother, Marybell had already suspected Ruben's honesty. She could not comprehend why it took so many years for him to visit, which made her anxious about other relationships he might have. Was that why he had not visited her children more often? In a way she was partly to blame, because her childhood love for Ruben was stronger than she made believe. She could not bring herself to cut herself loose from the clutches of a man who clearly did not show enough care for her and the children. Having spent most of her life trusting him, it was natural for her to hang onto the promise he had made during their courtship, that they would become man and wife. Ruben was a smart operator who knew how to keep the pretence alive, knowing that she and the children were not his only family. Yet, all this time Ruben was already married and had seven children by his other wife, plus many others dotted around the places he visited. Marybell was carrying a burning torch that could not easily extinguished, making his poor performance acceptable, enough to overlook any acts of misgivings. It is said that love is blind, and it is maybe so if you do not want to see the truth. If Marybell had known then that her decision would wrench the heart and soul of Ruben's friends and propel her son Lafty into a life of pain and suffering, it is doubtful she would have given him away. Marybell's fears had driven her to trust the man she loved, but did she really know him? The result of his actions condemned her to a life sentence of guilt. Could anyone blame a parent for wanting the best for their child, especially in a world where oppression dictated the destiny of the poor and under-privileged? Decisions such as that affecting Lafty will always be made, leaving a millstone for the unfortunate parent or both.

Ruben saw Lafty's cares differently to that of his mother. Lafty was not from Ruben's household; and did not carry the same genes as the children of Ruben's marital family. Lafty could have been anyone else's child, because Ruben's visits did not make him feel that he was his true father. Furthermore, he had not taken the time necessary to know his son, let alone to create a fatherly connection. The fact that Ruben had accepted Lafty as his son was a mere formality, and not an act of conviction. Ruben's appetite for adventure was probably more urgent, because he was easily steered away from the bonding that usually developed between families. He had exchanged the serenity of family life for the excitement of new horizons. But this time it had left his son desolate, and his good friend Mud perplexed.

Night swiftly took hold and the heat of a hot, sunny day gave way to the cool of the night breezes that help to freshen the irritating, foul smells that blanketed the ship. Mud in the meantime had long passed his meal time. The trauma of the evening had spoiled his appetite, and in its place Lafty's future became priority. It had been four hours since Ruben had told him of Lafty's arrival and by then Lafty would have spent many hours travelling and waiting. So once again Mud asked, 'Are you hungry, lad?' hoping Lafty would say yes, so that he too could grab a bite. Out came this quavering tune from what seemed a muffled voice with no spoken words, sending shockwaves through his head. He wondered what he could do for the boy. He was caught between being a kind person and an adult who could not apply any form of discipline. After all, discipline played the key role in a child's life, but Mud was restricted from doing anything that could be interpreted as anything other than kindness.

Lafty was like his father in hiding the truth. Could he ever become as devious as his father? He was carrying a secret, that he was in fact hungry. He had not eaten since the early hours of that morning, some ten hours ago, long before his arrival at the quayside. He had led Mud to believe that his mother had given him bread, which he had eaten during the journey, but it had only been a polite way to refuse food from a stranger, a practice his mother had taught him. But going without food was not Lafty's greatest fear. He loved his mother, and would not do anything to make her look or feel anything other than a good mother. She was always there, to the detriment of his absent father. Her lead was his only guide and he believed everything she taught him. When she told him that she loved him, nothing or no one could change his mind from believing that she was telling the truth. So why had she put him into the situation in which he found himself? Questions buzzed around his brain. Did she stop loving me? Should I despise her or carry on loving her memory? There were no easy answers.

The needle-sharp ends of the straw-filled mattress were no longer hurting. Lafty's disappointment had left his body numbed and in shock. He had been let down by the one person he loved more than any other and it was more than he could take. Shrouded in feelings of helplessness, he could not think straight. Everything pointed to his mother, and the question kept rolling over and over in his head. Why? As the swells of the mighty ocean waves crashed against the ship, echoing through the cabin, it was all he could think. The swell set off the squashing joints of the wooden beds and, accompanied by the orchestral creaking sounds of an ageing ship, brought torment to the mind of a frightened boy. The warmth of Mud's body was comforting and, for a time, brought refuge to the boy's soul. It also helped Lafty to dismiss any thoughts that Mud was a cutthroat, and that he was someone's meal, unlike many of the bedtime stories he had heard, which turned strangers into monsters. It felt good to be held by a father figure, something that had been missing from the twelve-year-old's life.

Having been good a father, Mud knew the importance of fatherhood to a frightened child, and upheld his responsibilities. After all, on his return home his family would be looking forward to those qualities. Lafty was one of the unfortunates who were denied a luxury that many children took for granted. His mother had fired his imagination by painting pictures of the exciting, exotic places in the world that Ruben had visited, and making him know that one day he, too, would share in the splendour of his father's experiences. Over the years Marybell had steadily built up the boy's readiness to experience something that was foreign to her. Lafty was her baby boy, bubbling with the energy of a young inquisitive brain that was yearning to learn and grasp anything that bore the slightest similarity to the imagery of his father. He had seen how other children interacted with their fathers and was overwhelmed. All he wanted was the same for himself, which was every boy's dream. When it did not happen, he was astounded and could not understand why he could not do the same. He could not separate the reality of his world from the burdened pretence of his mother's world. Maybe she thought she was doing something good. It is true that she had shed tears of sorrow, but was it because she had embedded her son's happiness in her dreams that it was about to become her greatest nightmare? The stories she told Lafty had been a sham because at no time could she with any certainty tell Lafty where his father was or when he was expected home. Ruben was always at sea, with no set plan of when he would arrive home, if ever. And all the time the little boy grew as the wait went on. For twelve years Lafty clutched onto his mother's words.

He had been four years old when he had first recognised his father and the experience had not left any lasting memories that could serve him well enough throughout the following eight years. In a quirky sort of way she could have been forgiven in painting those misleading pictures, because up until then Lafty could have passed his father in a crowd and would not have known who he was. Marybell had used those years to set the boy's brain alight and now his future was in the hands of a stranger and a father he barely know.

Mud had done a wonderful job in keeping Lafty calm. He had hoped that while Lafty settled, Dusty would walk through the door and give him the time to finish his wash. Dusty, he thought, was just the man to bring back a bit a sparkle to Lafty's eyes and a smile to his paling cheeks. The boy needed a bit of stimulation, he thought, something fresh and funny to take his mind away from this depressing environment and give him a reason to laugh.

Mud looked at the dark skin of his hands and legs and was stunned at the dried-on greasy coal dust that had formed strips and taken the appearance of retreating sands on the sea shore that and felt ashamed. Though he had decided not to leave Lafty until someone came, his condition would not be appreciated by Ruben or any of the others. If they walked into the cabin and saw him sitting in this darkened place with a strange twelve-year-old boy in my arms, they would think the worst of him.

However, regardless of what anyone might think, he had no intention of leaving Lafty on his own. His emotions were too volatile for him to be left alone. Come on home Dusty, Mud prayed. At no other time had he wished more for Dusty's presence. At the same time the ship was teasing them. As quickly as she levelled out, her violent actions would reoccur. She would roll, her keel making every move that a keel could. This was not good for Lafty or any loose objects. Whatever was not tied or bolted down would slide from side to side. Maybe the sea was sending Lafty a warning that he could not understand. Or maybe the ship was saying, 'Go home, little boy, you are not wanted here.' Her rocking–rolling motion agitated the boy's mind and sent his stomach dancing to a different tune. Locked in the arms of a half-naked man, his brain was dazed, temporary paralysis seized his feet, and his rumbling gut bubbled. He was helpless. But the ship had no concern for his feelings and continued its playful gestures, one minute it gently flattening out, and the next it caused sudden jolts, making Lafty spew another load. No wonder Mud's mug was so badly chipped.

Lafty was not the only one affected by this traumatic episode. Mud, too, was submerged by the pressure that the unexpected had brought. His body was crying out for sustenance and his brain needed a break. He has been working since the early hours of day, without a break, because Ruben hadn't been there to fulfil his obligation. Then when he had arrived he had bamboozled his friend Mud into caring for a young stranger, which had certainly tested his patience, not to mention the worrying condition of the old seadog, Dusty. His lateness was not making things any easier for Mud. Dusty had not seemed his usual chirpy self when they had parted earlier that evening, so his late return created a big stir. It was unusual for Dusty, who was always on time. Furthermore, he had been told of Lafty's arrival and the importance of his presence.

He also knew Ruben was working through the night. Mud's worried mind began to reflect on their parting. Dusty had been unsteady when he had tried to straighten up. Could his legs have given way, causing him to fall over and injure himself? His hopes were raised as echoing footsteps filled the gangway, and got closer to the cabin, but were dashed as they passed the door.

Mud tried to unravel the reasons for Dusty's condition. He was confident that Dusty did not drink while he worked; moreover there had been no smells of his favourite drink, rum. And, as far as he was aware, there had been no upsetting messages from Dusty's family. He was left puzzled. There was no easy way of finding out whether or not Dusty was feeling ill and was too afraid to tell someone. After all, nobody on board ship complained of their aches and pains. Mud could recall the time when Dusty broke his shoulder and did not tell anyone for weeks, and the recollection made him even more concerned for his friend and shipmate. He wanted to go and look for Dusty, but Lafty was his priority, he had to stay. So once again Mud began to wonder if Dusty had had a drink that day. With no logical answer he began to doubt his friend's honesty. There was always a first time, he thought.

Deep in thought, perplexed by the day's events, Mud took a good look at his half-washed, partly-dressed body, and the distressed boy curled up beside him. What if Ruben should turn up? What sort of message was this picture sending out? He had always been the toughest in the gang, but today he was no harder than a soggy bar of soap. It would be difficult to explain, especially to a gang that took pride in turning simple situations into catastrophic embarrassment.

Ruben and Mud shared a unique pastime, the love of beautiful ladies, and their pleasure had resulted in the birth of several children, some of whom they might have seen no more than once or twice in their lifetime. They were both married men with large families living on one of the most beautiful islands in the Caribbean

Sea. People described the island as a paradise. Those who got the opportunity to visit it soon found the description truthful. Mud was proud of his wife and seven children, though how many other children he might have had scattered around the islands were anyone's guess. He was a family man who spent one month in every six at home with his family. During this month he would form that father-child bond and get to know the different attitudes of each of his children. His behaviour would change drastically while he was with his family; no womanising or heavy drinking and most certainly no fighting. When those four men got home, their conduct was such that they were look upon as men of impeccable honour. Given the lifestyle they lived across the sea, the changes they made at home were extraordinary. The question was how did they do it? They were strong, tough, disciplined men who always seemed in control of their actions.

A comforting hug meant he was doing nothing less than carrying out his fatherly role. But Mud's physical appearance was that of a concrete pillbox, solid as an over-baked brick, the quality he needed to become a sailor. Working in the engine room was a job he loved dearly, though he had been given the chance to master various other jobs, despite not having the necessary qualifications. He was adored by his wife and children and with that happy-go-lucky personality he possessed his return would be greatly anticipated. His family would glow with happiness, which he attributed to their acceptance of his sailor's lifestyle. Many wives had considered the possibility of their husband having a lady friend in other ports, as Mud could wherever he went, but that did not matter, because love was what they had, and attention was what he gave. His homecoming days were an ocean of happiness. He would make his family feel special, as though they were only the people in his life, giving them confidence which made their lives complete. The children would be proud of their father's conduct, and see him as the perfect father.

Having created a near-perfect family relationship it became difficult for Mud to accept the separation of Lafty from his mother and sister. It was impossible to think objectively about the plan Ruben had hatched for his son, Lafty. It made him wonder if Ruben was treating his son in the same way as their grandparents had been treated by the slave masters. But if Ruben was taking Lafty to meet his half-brothers and sisters and there was no other plan then the journey could be in the boy best interests.

It would appear that a rift was being created among friends. Their willingness to help was not in question; Lafty's future was. The gang had repeatedly rejected any involvement in the selling or condoning of slavish acts so Mud quickly dismissed any ideas that his best friend was going to auction his son. Failing to secure an objective view of his best friend, Mud's brain was awash with uncertainties that had created doubts where there had been none. And for the first time the threads of trust that bound their friendship was being stretched to bursting. Shrouded with embarrassment his confused mind was forced to question their relationship, as he repeatedly asked himself, 'Do I really know my friend Ruben?' If only Ruben had shared his plans with his friends, Mud would have been better prepared to deal with the frightening display of Lafty's fears. His hands were tied. He did not know whether Ruben's plan was in Lafty's best interests or just another of his selfish whims. Ruben was known as Mr Charmer, the great manipulator, who was always hatching up half-baked plans. And he was very good at convincing his friends to support him without questioning his intentions. His compelling charm would work every time without. Ruben was looked upon as the leader, a position they had willingly accepted. And though they were grown men, they still cultivated childish, fun loving attitudes. Ruben being the master of spontaneity could dream up whims that supplied them with a continuous flow of excitement. That behaviour had become a way of life. Only an act of devastating proportions could change what they believed were the best years of their lives.

Draped in sadness Mud's eyes scanned the cabin, as if he was seeing it for the first time. The dark, painted walls that were dull and uninviting; rough wooden planks crudely nailed together as beds, one on top of the other, dressed with straw-stuffed sugar bags sown together as mattresses; shelves made to look like cupboards to hold their belongings, it was a sight that made his heart shiver in fear, fear that what he had seen might become part of Ruben plan. On reflection, though, Mud could remember the serious conversations they had had on their children's future. They had agreed then that neither of them would ever encourage their sons to become a sailor.

It was now way past the time when Dusty should have finished working, and Mud could have done with Dusty's help. How wonderful was the way in which those men carried out their duties. Each had their own way with jobs and attitudes, yet they entrusted their lives to each other without question. They were always lurking, constantly expressing a happy-go-lucky attitude. Little did they know that it was about to be curtailed by the seriousness of Lafty's dilemma. It had force Mud to take and look closely at his own life. He realised that he was no longer a young man, and that this trip could be his last journey on an unforgiving sea. And Lafty's situation was raising daunting questions that has been eating away at him on the inside, stirring a mood of sadness, even anger. 'What if one of these unscrupulous people should take away one of my boys?' he asked himself. 'What would I do? And how would my son feel? Would he feel the same as Lafty?' Mud was too anxious to think rationally, he could not make an objective judgement as to how his boy would feel nor how he would react, but Lafty had shown a kind of fear that had engaged his attention and made him more aware of the distress his own child could have been subjected to.

Shadowed by irrational thoughts one hour sitting with Lafty seemed like an eternity. He felt more tired during that one hour than he done he had done throughout his long working day from the early hours of that morning. Not only was he anxious to see Dusty, he was also nervous of what his reaction might be; after all he was half dressed, cuddling a strange boy, bad for his reputation. Regardless of what Dusty might think when he turned up, he would have to listen to Mud's explanation though he knew he would make a joke of it, further compounding his embarrassment.

With nothing more urgent to think of, Mud allowed his thoughts to wander to when he had almost fallen victim to the scheming of one of his many lady friends. The ship had docked and, after a long thirsty day they embarked on a wild night of fun sampling the delights of the shoreline establishments, enjoying the pleasures of beautiful loose women. No one gave a thought to the consequences of their outlandish behaviour, but on one such occasion Mud's night of excitement had given him the biggest scare of his life, and it was not until some years later that the seriousness of what happened was manifested. Whether it was good or bad luck, his past caught up with him.

So, the ship had docked and together the four mates were the untouchables: Mr Charmer Ruben, Mud and his two fighting machines, Dusty and Scruffy. The rum was flowing disgracefully, the women were plentiful and their macho egos were as high as a kite. A ramshackle building housed the rum bar, a shocking place. The holes in the roof were big enough to count the stars, and the gaps in the walls, not only for fresh air, were wide enough to serve the drinks through. Every inch of its dirty and dingy space was taken up by a crowded bunch of the good, bad and the indifferent. The atmosphere was electric and no sooner had they entered the place than the drinking and flirting had begun. Mud and his friends came alive as they celebrated their happiest times.

Without a care or concern, the drinks soon began to take effect. Soon Mud was in high spirits, lapping up the vibrancy of those promiscuous people as they latched onto any exposed weakness, and allowed their body language to do the talking. He felt a gentle kiss on the back of his neck, and fingers like velvet stroking his hair. Mud was being caressed like never before and was in the middle of a heavenly game. The warmth of a woman's body ignited his soul and set his heart in a rage of excitement. He turned to see who it was that was making him feel that way and saw an old flame. By then the rum was really taking a hold, and the foul smell of body odour and the stench of rotten vegetation, animals' and human's excrement had become the sweetest smelling perfume a lady could wear. This could be a long evening, he thought.

Mud had not seen this woman for many years. Indeed he hardly recognised her at first glance. The heat from the crowded rum bar and the energy of the alcohol sent the sweat pouring from his face. In a smooth and delicate motion, she gently wiped each trickle on his cheek and her passion reached his soul. It had been a dance on their first date that had captured his heart, and since then, she had been reeling for that moment to return. She wanted to repeat the dance.

Huddled together in the far corner with the stars for their lantern and tree trunks for chairs, talented musicians played their home-made instruments. A comb and paper, a fife made from the hollow bamboo, and the dry calabash husk filled with grains, harmonised the scintillating melody of the drums' infectious sound. With a steady flow of drinks from appreciative customers such as Mud and the others, the hypnotic vibes of those crudely made instruments and the potent effect of the alcohol raised the atmosphere to fever pitch.

The woman's presence was magic and Mud became ecstatic. His body was ablaze, and his eyes sparkled as he watched the movements of her beautifully curved body manipulating his excited brain without shame. She felt confident that a few more drinks of rum and Mud would succumb to her seductive plans.

She knew just which buttons to press to set Mud's body alight, and leave him powerless to her demands. So she danced his favourite tune, and her gyrating hips brought back memories he thought were lost. The excited Mud seized the bait she had set for him.

The place was as rough as its toxic smells suggested and the deafening noise made it the perfect haunt for con-artists. They thrived on the vulnerable, on visitors and on each other. Having spent months without their wives and days confined to the danger-ous working conditions at sea, every moment of this dream seemed to the sailor like an adventure, and was precious to their soul. A willing woman, plenty to drink and a good fight was the tonic a sailor needed. It helped to release the tensions created by an ocean of wilderness.

The wench was in no mood to compromise. She seized her chance and went for the kill. Her plan was to get Mud to take respon-sibility for her son. The smell of her perfume and the taste for rum seduced his brain, and made Mud listen to the wench's words. But they were a shocking surprise and caught Mud unprepared. Drunk he might have been, but he was no fool. Mud said yes to the wench's plan, and she became ecstatic. Filled with joy, she had won. Over she went and whispered to Dusty, 'I've got him at last. A father to my son!'

Hearing what she said, Dusty was enraged knowing that Mud had not seen this wench for years. After all, her child could have been the son of any of the many men she had presumably met. Drunk as he was, it was time for the fun to begin. With no set rules and not a referee in sight, the biggest fight you would ever hope to see broke out. With flailing arms Mud and his shipmates busily defended all sailors from the clutches of wenches who prey on their pockets. What a night, he thought, and what a lucky escape from a situation that could have haunted his life.

As memories of that night pulverised his mind and the reality of his present again became clear, he began to see things differently. The violence and uncertainty that dogged a sailor's life should not be what Ruben wanted for his son. They had lived the experience and were fully aware what that life could be for the boy. That made him more determined to discourage his son from becoming a sailor, though Lafty's future was his immediate concern. Even though he knew that being a sailor could quickly make a man out of a boy, it was not the right future for his son or Lafty. He was aware that children from poor families had a limited choice of career. Which career his son would be capable of was unclear then, but he knew he would never encourage either one of his sons to become a sailor. He realised they would have to work at something, a trade or otherwise, but hoped it would be something that might offer them a better lifestyle, especially if either one should take on the responsibilities of creating a family.

These few minutes were of tremendous help to Mud. They made him become more resolute about helping his sons towards a better future. No one wanted to have their son taken away to become a slave, or work in slavish conditions, a treatment that many poor people were forced to accept. Not only were they poor, they did not have the right to express their views or their wishes. And Mud was planning to steer his family away from that situation and help them to become stronger. But how, he wondered?

Mud had been working the seas for as long as he could remember, and had lost the will to farm the smallholding his parents left him. Moreover, he was no longer a young person. He did not know enough about farming to keep the family in the lifestyle to which they had grown accustomed. Working at sea was all that he knew. It would break his heart to leave the many friends he had made and loved over the years, but his choice was limited because age was against him. It was a decision he would have to make at sometime and Lafty's plight helped him to see it objectively.

Although slavery had long been abolished by English law, and some masters of large plantations had returned to their homeland, the agents that were left to conduct their business would only allow the law to become effective if doing so was to their advantage. It took a long time and hundreds of lives were to be lost before the changes were recognised and observed. The Maroon Treaty of 1838 in Jamaica, granted by the King George, set a small but significant group of slaves free from the bondage of those large plantation owners. The indignity that slavery created was the driving force that had caused Lafty's mother to take and made that decision.

Having been a sailor, Mud could enjoy a better quality of freedom than many of those who worked the land. Even though he was enslaved to the ship's masters, he could drink, get drunk, womanise and enjoy a good fight. But the sailors' freedom was based on a despicable inhumane premise, because it was entirely to the benefit of their employers. And only the lucky few, or the most intelligent, got the chance to excel and enjoy some sort of respect from their employer. Mud hope that his son would become one of the few with a choice, one who would not have to accept the lifestyle he might otherwise be compelled to adopt.

Lafty's dilemma had certainly opened his mind and allowed his thoughts to wander freely, and empowered him to survey the complexity of a new world that was far different to the one he had taken for granted. He had been given a rare opportunity to examine someone else's plight, which alerted his eyes to his own environment, prompting many questions. Mud was forced for the first time to accept the kind-natured person he was, a challenge to the perception of him as one of a tough bunch. If his dream were to become a reality, he could be grateful to Ruben's ill-fated ideals, because it had helped him to see that he was not that much better than his good friend. Even though he could read better than many others, it was easy to recall how difficult it had been to become a sailor. Becoming a sailor catapulted his brain into recognising the true value of education. It gave him the chance to travel outside the country of his birth and the opportunity to experience the good, bad and indifferent, which was invaluable when reaching a decision. If he was to achieve his goal and ensure his sons had choices beyond the lifestyle of a sailor, he would have to think and plan more responsibly than his friend Ruben.

The result of his soul-searching help him to set a course, his priority now was to provide the building blocks for his children. Whether he lived or died at sea, it was no longer as important as the educated future he wanted for them. But, he wondered, had Ruben thought of Lafty in the way he was now thinking of his sons? He prayed that Ruben would not commit Lafty to the perils of the sea, and their inexcusable lifestyle.

Time was ticking away; colourful language filled the gangway as sailors returned from an exhaustingly long day. It was not the type of welcome he wanted for Lafty, especially at such a delicate time and his nerves twitched. The boy was in an alien world surrounded by strange faces, and was compelled to accept a situation that would have been frightening for many adults, let alone a child. His limp body was desperate for the comforting arms of his mother and all he could think of was home with his family. He did not know the meaning of incarceration, but Mud was sure that was how it must have felt to him. This journey was supposed to be an adventure. Or at least that was what the boy would have been told by his mother. His little brain would have been working overtime, recalling childhood dreams of becoming a sailor and sailing the mighty seas. How their little hearts must have raced with excitement. But where was the excitement now?

His giant muscles tensed as he held tightly to what seemed a fragile piece of porcelain, and brought peace to Lafty's troubled mind. The warmth of his body made the boy feel safe; safe enough to loosen his rigid thoughts and send them cascading into free fall, to wander merrily through his childhood days. Many of his friends, whom he could name, had parents as poor as his mother. They could not read, or spell their names, although counting from one to twenty and reciting the alphabet from A to F had been easy. What little education they had enjoyed had been given at the mission school miles from their homes and after paying the teacher, either with money or in kind. Lafty's mother had not been able to pay regularly; she did not have a farm or a steady job. And Lafty could only attend school when someone took pity on her situation and gave her a day's work, and if there was enough money to spare he could enjoy a day out at school.

Everyone had gone to church on Sunday. The tiny building would be packed. There were more children than the space allowed, so they were squashed together like sardines in a tin and made to sit on wooden planks. Quietly, they sat and listened, hoping for the day when they too became adult men and women. But it had not all been bad. Lafty remembered the teachers were very energetic and they taught the children almost every Bible story that they could understand, using words and pictures of trees, fruit, birds, animals, buildings, mountains and valleys, or anything that the children would have seen during their daily lives. Many of those stories were still fresh in his head and Lafty would use his fantastic memory to tell Bible stories, leaving many people amazed, and wondering where he had learnt to read and write.

Lafty was a listener who could retain information. Most of his friends had not been as fortunate. The majority of them lived within the confines of the plantation, and were subjected to strict discipline; guidelines by which they lived, with set times when they could play or attend school. Failure to obey was punishable either with the belt, a whip or, in some cases, they were locked away or placed in some desolate corner and made to go without food. But those children had been his friends; they were tough, strong and kind-hearted. And when they had played together they had had fun. As his thoughts wandered deeper into the past, he was forced to accept that he was about to share their plight. His situation was no better, because he, too, was locked away – on a darkened ship, among strangers.

CHAPTER 6

Friendly Faces

Lafty had been born outside the protection of the big plantation and its punishing slavish discipline. His life was miles of hunger, and yards of raggedy play. He was a boy who no one had reason to think of. He was nothing special; in fact he was probably the opposite, not even enough to warrant sympathy for the way in which society treated black, poor, weak and vulnerable people. However, his freedom had its limits. Its restrictions tormented his mother and made her desperate to break loose from its shackles. He had no way of knowing the reasons for her actions; no one had told him that his life might be different, if he was given the opportunity to choose. The subject of slavery was rarely discussed and if it was, it was done away from the ears and eyes of children.

Lafty's body trembled at the thought of punishment. He was fearful that he would be punished at some time, more likely beaten, either by his father or an elder, and was banking on the kindness he saw in Mud's caring eyes. If he was going to beat him, Lafty thought, Mud would have done it by then. Mindful of his wishes, Lafty was trapped in a world of heartfelt maybes, without choice. He had shed enough tears, he thought. It seemed the right time to trust Mud's caring words and deeds. He had learnt an extraordinary lesson of faith from his friends, which made it easy to acknowledge and accept Mud's friendship. They had faith in their parents' assurances that one day they could be free of the bondage they had endured. And the knowledge he had gained strengthened the trust he held for his father, and gave him courage to trust in Mud's kindness. But, at the same time, he hoped that his father would hasten his return.

Half-dressed, his hands and face bearing the scars of his working environment, and colourfully decorated by rejected contents of Lafty's stomach, Mud looked like an African warrior about to take his place in a tribal ceremony. In truth he was more fearful of his mates' cynical jibes at his predicament. He could stick it out no longer and swiftly but gently lay Lafty on the bed and scrambled to the wash area hoping that no one saw him. He had broken the promise he had made never to leave Lafty on his own. And he could have done with Dusty's help. Mud was not a practising Christian, but he was remorseful for his actions and so began to offer a prayer to God.

'Please God,' he said, 'let no one see me like this. Not while I'm running away from a crying boy. I'd never hear the last of it. I would die if they thought badly of me. And while you are at it, God, let the boy stay quiet until I return.' Mud, the big, strong giant of a man, was as frightened as a defenceless child, probably more so than Lafty. He hurriedly made his way, behaving like an escape convict, filled with suspicion, looking around every corner, hoping that no one spotted his caveman-style appearance. Heart in overdrive, he darted to the wash place so fast his feet hardly touched the floor. But Dusty and Scruffy were already there, having a whale of a time. When he saw them, Mud was dumbstruck, and for moment did not know what to do or say. He was disappointed that his prayers had not been answered in the way he would have liked. Maybe God thought they could all do with a bit of a laugh to dispel some of the gloom and despair that had dogged their lives.

He thought right, because the mocking and teasing was instant, and went far beyond what he had expected. He was embarrassed at the reception given to him by his best friends, it was far worse than what he might otherwise have received from his other workmates.

He had also arrived at the right time, right for Dusty and Scruffy that is. Their light-hearted take on what was clearly a very distressing time for Mud, and he was forced to act the slave for his friends just to keep them quiet for a while. He was made to fill buckets of seawater to wash their grease-stained bodies, and to endure their provocative chants. Distraught at Lafty's burden and confused by the secrecy of Ruben's plans, Mud's calm and placid persona was shattered. That evening he had burdened himself with a mountain of guilt as he had contemplated the speed at which he had to accept changes; changes that made it impossible for him to explain away his awful looking appearance.

There was no privacy while washing or performing toiletry functions. Sanctuary was confined to a small open space at the ship's bows, where all acts of sanitation were carried out with the aid of seawater. Furthermore, at that time the place was overrun by other sailors all forging a link with nature. Mud could only wait for the right moment to tell his friends about Lafty's presence, and about Ruben's secret plan. This time Ruben's plans had far exceeded anything Mud was prepared to tolerate. Conditions might have been suitable for hardened sailors, but it certainly was not right for an innocent country boy with no sailing experience.

Amid the laughter, leg-pulling and the dangling buckets of seawater, Mud tried desperately to explain what had turned his appearance into that of a badly painted statue. But his fun-loving friends' jeering drowned the seriousness of his encounter. Mud was upset at the insensitive attitude of his good friends. He could not erase the picture in his mind of Lafty's limp body curled on the bed and it suddenly unlocked a reservoir of tears.

Dusty and Scruffy were bemused; their smiling faces turned as blank as a sheet of paper and their laughter came to an abruptly halt, leaving the two men speechless. Mud could sympathise with Scruffy's behaviour, because he was unaware of Lafty's arrival, but he was very unhappy with Dusty's attitude. Dusty, the man whose health he had been worried about, was as bright as a silver button. He knew that Lafty was on board yet he was making it difficult for Mud to give a rational explanation for his wearied looks.

As the tears receded, so did Dusty's and Scruffy's mocking. Mud and Dusty had to remind Scruffy of the promise they had made Ruben a long time ago. Like the others Scruffy, too, had forgotten. Ruben was always coming up with ideas that no one took seriously. But confused as he was, Scruffy could clearly recall Ruben suggestion; it had been made after a night of high-spirits in one of many seedy rum bars they frequented, not the ideal time or place to make a promise about something as important as caring for Lafty.

Scruffy listened to Mud's concerns for Lafty, who could have been either one of their sons, and the realisation dawned that he was soon to become a nursemaid for Ruben's selfish plans. This made him angry, but it was too late to show anger; Lafty was already on board, traumatised and distressed. Mindful of the boy's situation, the three men agreed to put their angry feelings aside, and make the little boy's journey as comfortable as they possibly could. The three of them exchanged apologies and reassured Mud that their frolicking had been just a bit of harmless fun and their friendship was as strong as ever. They hugged each other and rekindled the inseparable bond they had forged between them. Each began to acquaint himself to the prospect of their new cabin mate and the urgency of their promise. They quickly washed and changed into something less dirty in readiness for Lafty. Regardless of Ruben's plans, they thought, Lafty would become their priority. Filled with compassion for the little boy's plight Mud, Dusty and Scruffy affirmed their pledge to make sure Lafty had a fair deal; three determined men, ready to make right what they could. They hastily went to the cabin, where the sad-looking Lafty sat coiled like a snake, awaiting the next move.

Mud had experienced Lafty's outburst, and was silently wishing there would be no repeat. Along the darkened gangway the water dripped from their bodies. The haunting sounds of a ship that seemed displeased sounded menacing, and Mud thought that if Lafty was still awake, then the presence of Dusty and Scruffy frighten him more, and there was no way of telling what he might do. As their gentle steps reached the cabin's door they found a scared little boy, awaiting his destiny. He had been left alone far longer than he should have been, so he looked a sorrowful sight. They thought of their own children having to go without the reassuring cuddles of their mother's arms, and took courage in carrying out their promise. One by one, with smiling faces, they entered the little boy's domain, hoping he stayed calm and accepted them as his friends.

Lafty had had plenty of time during Mud's absence to look around and listen to the varying sounds that surrounded him, many of which he could not recognise. But he could hear voices and the crashing of feet on what seemed like a waterlogged floor. Maybe the ship had sprung a leak, but what could he do? His only option was to settle his mind to his conditions and hope that something good would happen and someone would come and take him back to his mother. He believed that Mud could be trusted, and that strengthened his confidence. Mud could become his hero, and help him return home. It was time that Lafty put his thoughts to the test and accepted Mud's friendliness.

As quiet as they were, Lafty could hear their footsteps and was alerted to their entry. His partially closed eyes watched their giant feet getting closer, while his motionless body curled into an uncomfortable position. The dim light of the kerosene lantern gave the cabin a shadowy feel, making its appearance far worse than it would have been in daylight. His frightened body shook in fear not knowing what was about to happen. His heartbeat thundered, and he struggled for breath. Could the stories of cut-throats on the high seas be true, he wondered? His only comfort was the repeated promises Mud had made, that no one was going to hurt him, but that did not take away the fear that was racing through his mind. The overbearing suspense forced Lafty to open his eyes. As he did, his eyes collided with Mud's who was standing at his bedside looking on, feeling as nervous as Lafty.

'Thank goodness you are awake; we did not want to frighten you again. Now, I have something to tell you and I don't want you to feel afraid, or to worry. These two gentlemen are your father's and my friends, and they are going to help to look after you while you are on board this ship.'

Lafty bravely smile and as he did, the words came out, 'Thank you, sir.'

Mud was relieved to hear Lafty speak. 'Are you hungry, lad?' Mud asked.

Lafty shook his head in reply as if to say, 'No, sir.'

Dusty and Scruffy busied themselves drying the water from their hands and necks, with what looked like an old pair of shorts or some sort of rag. Mud sat on the bed, beside Lafty. His heart melted in shame as the emotion of his fatherly instinct took hold of his mind. He could have easily broken down into a flood of tears again but that would not have been of any help to Lafty. If Lafty was to be helped then Mud had to show strength and courage, and hope Lafty would follow his lead.

Mud slid his hands over Lafty's fragile body, gently stroking his head and shoulders and whispering in his ears, 'Everything is going to get better; don't you worry.'

Fine words they might have been, he thought, but where was the proof? After all, the man who brought Lafty here, who said he loved him, and who was supposed to protect him was nowhere to be seen. Could he be as trusting as he made believe?

Though Lafty thought, he understood what his father had meant when he had left him alone in that cabin and gone to commence his working shift, Lafty could be forgiven for becoming anxious and resentful of his father's friends. He was twelve years old and had never seen a floating ship before that day, let alone sailed on one. Lafty's love for his father was beyond bonds. He worshipped every word he spoke. One day, he thought, he could be just like his father. Lafty had moulded his future on the adventurous lifestyle that his father lived, even though he was too young to understand the dangers and disappointments that lurked amid adventure. But Lafty had not thought that the opportunity to emulate his father would present itself at such an early age. He wanted to fulfil those ambitions when he was grown up, not then. Why does everything have to be so complicated? he thought.

The three men who claimed to be his father's friends were strangers. They did not seem to fit the kind of fatherly figure he had imagined of his father, even though his only guide to his father's personality came from the stories his mother told of him, and the short encounter they had had before he decided to remove him from his mother and sister. Tears streamed down his cheeks, as thoughts of his family flashed through his head. But by then he had made up his mind to become a brave boy, in hope that the strangers, who promised friendliness, would see him as a good boy and spare him from beatings or cruel acts. Lafty quickly wiped the teardrops from his smooth, soft cheeks and presented a face that warmed his minders' hearts.

However, deep in side a volcano of fears rumbled, waiting to erupt. Lafty could have been experiencing similar fears as his mother, without knowing. Her fears had been of the faceless dictators who ruled the lives of the poor with an iron rod of cruelty. She had wanted to remove her son from the path of those impending obstacles but had she make the right decision? If she could have faced Lafty at that moment and explained to him the reason behind the decision she had taken on his future, would he have told her that she got it all wrong?

Lafty was a very happy child, who thought his mother, and the beautiful community in which he was brought up, was the best. But her decision to place him with his father had created resentment, and ignited entrenched feelings of betrayal. He was only twelve; not the age that could have equipped him with the knowledge to understand the difficulties that a parent faces.

A few deep breathes triggered a cascading steam of foul liquid, causing signalled his big brown eyes to pop, and his parting lips to smile, which finally put Mud's heart at ease. It was a very encouraging left Mud and his friends doubled up, laughing. Thank God, Mud thought, the boy is getting to like me; soon I'll get him to eat something. That would make me very happy. Once again Mud repeated his offer of food to Lafty, but yet again he refused to eat.

Although they were expressing friendly faces and spoke in a soft gentle tone, these men were strangers to Lafty, which made it difficult for him to trust either of them. It was the heavily concentration of rippling muscles and ragged appearances that made him fearful. He felt marooned in a ship on the open sea, where there was nowhere to run from the dark night-time sky and the angry roar of lashing waves, and home was miles away. He was not prepared to take food from any other hand than his father's. It was the only aspect of his life he was in control of and he was not ready to give it up.

The strong, stroking grips of Mud's arms made Lafty more relaxed. His worried mind became subdued and he fought back the tears. Lafty felt strong, as though he had awakened from his greatest nightmare. Mud's insistence on bringing calm to Lafty's troubled mind had paid off and the little boy was ready to accept the friendship of those men. His smiles widened and his tearless eyes shone like freshly cut, lighting up the beauty of his innocence. It was what Mud had been anxiously waiting for.An air of excitement filled the cabin. Each one looked at the other with joy, their faces aglow like a cluster of stars in a cloudless night. Mud was no longer worried. It was the first tangible sign of communication between them, which he hoped could develop into a strong and lasting friendship.

On that theme Mud wasted no time embracing the opportunity and lifted Lafty high off the bed. It was an instant transformation as Lafty became his bundle of joy. Mud began to brandish an infectious smile as he sat Lafty back down on the bed in an upright position.

'Now, lad,' he said, looking into Lafty's eyes.

Lafty was fearful of what Mud might say or do. Instead of listening to Mud, he had engaged with the movements of Mud's thick lips, giant nose and the horrible looking scar above his left eye. How did Mud get that scar? Lafty wondered. The bridge of Mud's nose seemed to have been flattened out, as if it had been hammered flat. His cheekbones protruded beneath the skin to form what looked like cress on a mountain peek. Lafty nervously quivered at Mud's hardened face.

Mud continued, 'Are you sure that you have eaten and are not feeling hungry? It's no trouble. I can soon go and get you something to eat.'

The boy shook his head violently, almost severing it from his shoulders. His moving lips were clear to see, 'No sir, I am not hungry, thank you, sir.'

Lafty's behaviour was not to Mud's liking; he felt sure Lafty was hiding the truth and was in fact hungry, but he could not force Lafty to eat.

'Would you like another drink of water, lad?' Mud asked.

The boy gestured, saying, 'Yes, please sir,' and this sent Mud leaping to his feet, so much so that the force of his giant muscles almost knocked Lafty clear off the bed. He grabbed the chipped, infested mug, darted through the tiny doorway, pushing aside his shipmates, and hurriedly went to fetch Lafty a drink of water. His feet were bare, he wore no shirt and had on a thick leather belt that was too wide to thread through the loops of his ragged trousers, but he had no concern as to what others might think or say about his appearance. His rippling muscles danced happily beneath his black skin as he skipped briskly down the narrow gangway, brandishing the smile of man who had inherited a fortune. He climbed up the steep steps to the water barrel. Mud was on a mission that was far more important than any other business; he had raised a little boy from his sadness. It was one of those rare moments that brought with it the elation of a good fight, especially one that ended without a broken bone.

Mud's rush to hasten what he thought was the first step to Lafty's acceptance, left Dusty and Scruffy bemused and wondering what had gone wrong, but Mud completed the journey in record time. To everyone's delight, especially Lafty's, his speed was astounding. Mud was too big to be so agile, he thought. Lafty had experienced Mud's absence on two occasions and in both cases, the wait had seemed endless. Mud handed Lafty the mug which was almost full. He had not spilt much in his dash, and there were only a few dead flies and pieces of woodchip floating in it, though it was perfectly safe to drink.

The refreshing breeze of the night air did little to dampen the warm temperature below deck, and the ship's cramped conditions made the cabin a suffocating and thirsty place for everyone. Lafty's appreciation of that mug of water could only be summed up in one mouthful. With eyes ablaze and smiles from ear to ear, Lafty took the mug and drank the water. 'Thank you, sir,' his opening mouth revealed.

Excitement filled the tiny cabin and by now a whole crowd of the crew had gathered round, glaring at the little boy like he was a priceless exhibit or the latest toy in a Christmas sale. And they shouted, 'We are your uncles, from here on in.'

Having sensed Lafty's burden, Mud was particularly pleased at the end of what had seemed a sad evening. His heart lightened as his tenacity had been rewarded with a vision of strength and courage, just what boy needed. Finally looking at himself and noting his bleak appearance in the presence of a strange and frightened little boy,

Mud reached for his clothing, a rag-like garment which only he could have described as a shirt. It was a shirt that did not look anything like a shirt. There were more holes in it than a fisherman's net, which Lafty found amusing, and for the first time his attention was fully engaged on something other than his own plight. His devilish thoughts allowed his true character to shine through, and exposed his cheeky sense of fun and laughter. Lafty began to behave like the happy child he had been within his natural and simplistic environment. He watched as Mud delicately slipped the shirt over those bulging muscles, careful not to create any extra holes. The harder Mud tried, the more the shirt tore. His smile soon turned into an entertainment, infusing the other sailors, and filling the cabin with a roar of infectious laughter. Lafty eyes were aglow with mischievous signals and his brain was overrun with thoughts of Mud's shirt.

'It's a new kind of air conditioning,' laughed Mud.

Lafty's smile was the smile of a happy child. It broke the silence and prized open Dusty's and Scruffy's joke box. Soon the ship's gangway echoed their fun and laughter. Mud's objective had been achieved. Lafty's behaviour was what he had expected of a twelve-year-old boy. Having lightened the atmosphere, the time was right for Dusty the clown to bring a touch of magic to proceedings and ignite the boy's playful nature. This, Mud thought, could remove any feelings of rejection that Lafty's brain might still be harbouring. But although Lafty was enjoying Dusty's funny moments, there was still a deep suspicion that the boy was consumed in self-pity and that a tactful approach was very important. While the little boy found laughter, Mud, Scruffy and Dusty gave their all to their jokes, and Lafty's ears were steadily bombarded with fun-loving stories, most of which manufactured in Lafty's interest. Some of these he would always remember, others were forgotten as quickly as they were heard. The laughter gave the sailors' routine a new lease of life, though Dusty's heart grew sad midway through his performance, wondering if Ruben would realise the severity of the damage he might have caused the boy.

The stillness of the night air and the crowded cabin full of sweating bodies raised temperature in the cabin, invoking a musty odour. The smell was that of a farmyard, an obnoxious irritant to the little boy's chest. But the cabin was buzzing with excitement as one by one they gave their renditions, filling the air with laughter, relieving the tension that sometimes ate away at their happy lifestyle. But the sailor's clothes were often funnier then the jokes they told and this brought light-hearted relief to Lafty's troubled mind. Dusty and Scruffy had returned to finish their wash, and changed into different clothing. Different it might have been, but cleaner it was not. It seemed the men had swapped one set of greasy, paint-stained clothes for another. And, that to Lafty was even funnier than the jokes he had heard. Mud's clothes had caused the biggest stir. The little boy thought it looked like a moonless sky, peppered with brightly lit stars with Mud's dark skin projecting the back-drop of a darkened sky. And, with his trousers flapping halfway up his legs, it looked like a dog had been chewing at them. Only the innocence of a child could strip away the seriousness of the situation, leaving a cabin full of smiling faces.

Slowly a different Lafty had emerged, showing far more courage than was expected. He had opened his mind and given acceptance to the mercy on the many faces and eyes that were crowding his space. Mud had made the boy feel safe, mindful that there were no guarantees that one of the other sailors would not take exception. After all Ruben, his father, was not there to give the support Lafty was entitled to. He was working and would not finish his shift for a few hours more. Lafty could only hope and pray that the trust he had put into Mud was justified and that Ruben's shift would end soon. His brain suddenly began to work like that of an adult; one half was convinced that Mud would make him safe, while deep inside his heart was quivering with fear at the thought of what kind of future awaited him. He was at the mercy of a father he did not know well, and there was nothing anyone could do to change it. Mud and his friends could help in making his life as comfortable as they could, but they could not change any decision his father intended to make or had already made.

Darkness overwhelmed the open sea, and the night began to dog his troubled mind. Feelings of hunger weakened his body while the turbulent movement of the ship seemed vengeful. His mouth became dry and, tired from laughter, chewing was a painful exercise. He thought of home, his mother, sister and friends, imagining what he would be doing if were there. He would be sleeping, or playing with his pet rabbit. Playing with his pet gave him pleasure and lots of comforting hours although it sometimes used to put him at odds with his mother when he stayed up late in the evenings. Maybe it was his fear of the dark that made Lafty so attached to his pet, but like all good mothers Marybell knew how to deal with his fears. At the first sign of darkness she would hurry him to bed, gently coaxing him into closing his eyes and going off to sleep before she put out the light. If she mistakenly put it out too quickly, it could end in tears. It was worrying to have been left in the dark, unable to sleep. Lafty's brain would become overloaded as the darkness took hold and gradually created imaginary problems in his troubled mind. At twelve no one would expect him to be afraid of the dark, especially in such close proximity to the other people who shared the same space. If only he was five years old again, his age could become an excuse for his weakness.

Mud had given Lafty love and attention and had even introduced him to his caring friends, but Lafty wondered how he could calm his fears. He began to put Mud's personality to the test. By doing so, he thought, he could restore the confidence he had in the man he hoped would help rescue him from his father's plans. Mud had presented a kind and understanding personality from the first time they had met, and had mentioned that he, too, was a father.

As Lafty's thoughts continued to meander, his body became limp and his lips slowly closed, obscuring the sparkle that had flashed from his brilliant white teeth.He had reached the limit of rational thought for a boy of his age and was desperate for the guidance of a grown-up. But how could he ask for it? What could he say and where should he start? He had been thrust into a situation that would have been depressing for a grown man, let alone a boy of twelve. He felt as though someone had dipped his naked body into a bucket of ice-cold water and left it shivering with cold. Locked in a strange time zone, with his dreams hanging by a weak thread, he felt helpless, dejected and fearful.

Mud and Dusty were popular for that rough, tough, ragged look, they never ran shy of a good fight, and could do most things, but they were also very sensitive men. They were very protective and kept a close watchful eye on Lafty, charting the changing movements of his face. Their jokes were wonderful and enjoyable but were not exactly suitable for a little boy desperate for his mother's love. Both men would periodically tightened their caring grip, reminding Lafty that they were there for him, and wherever his thought were taking him, they needed him to return and join them. They looked at each other and, without a word being said, they called a halt to the fun and laughter. After all, the noise was getting out of control, and so was the colourful sailor's language.

'Right me lads, its time for young Lafty, to get his beauty sleep,' said Mud. 'Say goodbye, my friends, and see you in the morning.' He lifted the boy onto the top bunk and covered him with a rough-looking cover. Like worker ants the crew members obediently soldiered through the door and down the gangway, their laughter slowly evaporating in the darkness. The sailors' absence brought relief to his minders. They had just about managed to protect the lad from the vulgarities that were part and parcel of a sailor's lifestyle. The cabin could just about sleep four and as Ruben's shift would not end until the following morning Lafty would be able to enjoy an uninterrupted rest. It was the best thing to have happened so far to Lafty since his arrival. He had peace of mind and his own space, which he would have had to share with his sister if he had been at home. Through the darkened space the three men looked at each other and, without saying a word, their thoughts were in perfect harmony. The gentle strokes of Mud's fingers smoothed Lafty's forehead and pulled back his thoughts from the abyss, inviting the little boy to join a band of men that he could trust and call his friends.

Lafty respond in a way that astonished the men. The boy suddenly changed, as if by some sort of magic his fears liquefied and turn into a pool of courage; enough to set off a lap of friendly smiles. In silence thought the men observed the young boy's movements and glowing facial expressions. It gave them pleasure, knowing that they had brought stability to a frightened twelve-year-old child. The evening had ended on a happy note for those men. It had stretched late into the night signalling a shortened rest for Mud who had an early start the following morning. Having covered Ruben's shift for the past three days a good night's sleep was important to a hardworking man and by then he was feeling tired and in need of a well-deserved rest.

If only Ruben would face up to his responsibility, he thought, instead of leaving it up to someone else like me, life could be a lot more relaxing. Mud thought deeply of the kind deeds he was carrying out for his friend and hoped that someone in the future would return the kindness in whatever form to his own family. It was also time for Lafty to settle down and have some rest, after the ordeal of an extraordinary day.

'Now Lafty, me lad, you are quite sure you don't need something to eat?'

Once again Lafty told Mud that he was full, although Mud had his suspicions. Even if Mud had brought Lafty something to eat the poor boy would not have been able eat any of it, as he simply could not swallow, not even his own saliva. The ship seemed to have vented its anger on Lafty's throat, and his stomach had become a bubbling whirlpool. He cried without tears, there were none left.

'Are you comfortable, lad?' asked Mud, the last concern for the boy's well-being before he slumbered to sleep.

Distressed and confused, Lafty hesitated; he did not know what to do say. Should he tell him the truth? he wondered. But the answer was no. He was going to be a man and men are brave people and so he would be brave. In a happy, cheerful voice Lafty mumbled, 'Yes sir.' The vibrant sounds from the little boy were pleasing to Mud, but deeply he struggled to accept Lafty's situation. Mud felt that Lafty was not as happy as he made believe. How could he be happy, Mud asked himself. He's bound to be missing his mother while his father's away. Furthermore, the dancing ship was playing havoc with his stomach. So no matter however much Lafty tried convince him otherwise, Mud knew he was feeling awful.

That night was Mud's greatest nightmare. Even though he wanted to, there was nothing more he could do for Lafty, apart from climbing into bed beside him, which was out of bounds. Without a clear instruction from Ruben on how to treat his son, Mud had done all he could that day, even though it was not enough to satisfy either Lafty's fears or Mud's fatherhood instincts. Hard work and a long shift had sent both Dusty and Scruffy snoring into another world. So much for their help, Mud thought.

'Time for us to sleep, Lafty. Close your eyes and remember I am here if you need anything. Don't be afraid to call me.'

'Yes sir,' the boy thought.

Though Mud was trying very hard to understand Lafty, his answers were very economical. 'Yes sir', 'No, sir' and 'Thank you, sir'. Mud had shown patience and the virtue of humility but he was not making many inroads towards Lafty's acceptance and the movement of the ship was not helping. Suddenly the cabin plunged into darkness. That was disaster to Lafty. He lifted his head, peeped through the dense cloud of darkness and was greeted by a faint light at the far end of the gangway, which was comforting to his tattered mind. At least the door of the cabin had been left ajar. But Lafty could not see anything or anyone in the cabin. He thought his nightmare had begun when his father had lifted him into the bus-cart, but in fact, his nightmare began there and then. Not only did he have the fear of darkness to overcome, but the ship had joined in what seemed like a conspiracy to take his life and there was nothing he could do to stop it. The frightening sounds of giant waves crashing against the ship echoed through the cabin. Survival signals rumbled through his brain, and reminded his weakened body there was no escape. A voice kept telling him he was not strong enough to swim in the sea and the ship could be flooded before he reached the deck. And, as if that was not enough, the howling wind joined forces with the sea. There was nowhere to run or to hide.All that he had was the memory of a harrowing story his mother had told both him and his sister many times over. Mindful that the storm was real, Lafty's mind was transported into a world of pretence.

CHAPTER 7

Fear and Suspicion

It was the story of The Crystal Bowl that he hoped would keep his brain fully occupied through the dark hours. It was told to his mother Marybell by her grandmother Maude, and Marybell had passed it on to her children, to Lafty and his sister Celene.

The Crystal Bowl, she said, was a family heirloom, believed to have had magical powers that weaved a spell across many generations. It had been handed down until grandmother Maude had become its proud owner.

'Maude took great delight in telling us grandchildren all about the magical powers of the crystal bowl," explained Marybell. 'Come nightfall, Grandma Maude would make sure we were well scrubbed, dressed and ready for bed. It would become a tussle to see who sat closest to hear the tales of her past. She knew that we would do anything to hear her story, so it was not difficult for her to get us to sit still.

'We would sit on the hard wooden floor, hugged together in a circle. The light from the oil lamp would make the beautifully polished floor sparkle and the silence would become deafening. We children would be seduced by fear, and would squeeze together so tightly that fresh air would struggle to pass in between us. Then Maude would lower her voice to almost a whisper and we would listen intensely. She would begin by telling us of the house in which she was born and brought up with her family.

'"It was a beautiful house," she said. "One of the biggest in our town. Some of my friends wished they had a house like ours. It had three bedrooms, a veranda, and was built from well-seasoned cedar wood with shiny sheets of zinc covering the roof. The wooden-blind windows were elegantly crafted, caught the sunlight and set the house apart from the rest. The house was shared by my family and my aunt's family."

'Grandma Maude's eyes would light up like a pair of burning candles as the story unfolded. "In the sitting room beneath the window," she'd tell us, "stood a wooden table that was polished to a shine that mirrored our faces. And in the centre of that elegant table was this magnificent heirloom, The Crystal Bowl. It was a beautiful thing that everyone loved and admired, and its diamond shapes were set ablaze by the bright sun, its surface smooth to the touch."

'Well, Grandma Maude told us that many years ago at midday, during a mid-summer month, a scary yet spectacular happening took place. She said, "I was twenty-two years old and my sister was twenty. That day the sun seemed to have reached melting point. No one had ever known it that hot. Even the stream where they collected water dried to a trickle, leaving the family with an endless thirst. Everyone looked forward to the setting sun and the approaching nightfall, when the temperature would become more bearable. But with so many of us sharing the home, by the time we began to feel comfortable, the sun would be rising and the agony would begin all over again. In the middle of what we thought was the hottest day a very unusual phenomenon took place, sending shockwaves that affected the lives of every individual in the family and disrupting family life near and far. The elegant Crystal Bowl projected images on the wall that created fear in their minds."

'It wasn't unusual for the crystals to cast shadows,' explained Marybell, 'which could form pictures of birds or plants or anything for that matter. However, on that day the Crystal Bowl cast a completely different picture. It was so lifelike it was scary and people became too frightened to dismiss its realism. The picture, Maude told us, was that of a hanging lady.

'Hearing this, we children were almost too scared to move. The atmosphere in the room was gripping. "I was very frightened," said Maude.

'News of the picture quickly reached every family, and created enormous excitement and superstition. It gave people lots to talk about and they made predictions as to the validity of the picture. They thought it was the sign of a curse, which suggested that someone within the family was about to meet an untimely death or fall ill at the very least. Each person looked at someone else for somewhere to lay the blame. When they could not find anyone they began to search their own consciences for any wrongdoings. This story was hot news; it had all the ingredients for a good gossip. Nothing like this had ever happened in this sleepy town before the picture of the hanging lady had appeared to them and it was something to be amazed and anxious about. More than anything, they wanted to see this mysterious picture."

'As Grandma Maude stared at our faces she saw our eyes were ablaze with excitement, so much so that our tender skin had become wet and sticky. "Like you," she said, "there were lots of worried people in the village who were convinced that something bad was about to happen to someone in the family. Their fearful anxiety triggered off a lot of superstitious talk that black magic was to blame. They believed that someone in the family was dealing in witchcraft, and a witch should be found to rid them of this evil curse. A lot of trust was lost between families and within the community, but no one was named for the wicked deeds."'

Marybell went on, 'Maude told us the story became a wild fire out of control, affecting everyone's belief. Not surprisingly, while the news rapidly spread, one or two details of the story changed, making it more dramatic. At one point the story had changed to a lady actually hanging herself in the house. This awakened a great curiosity, and our house had more than its fair share of visitors that summer, hoping to see the picture of this hanging lady. Maude said,

"As children we, too, would make excuses to stay in the house with the visitors cramped inside the tiny room, hoping to catch a glimpse of the sun shining on the Bowl. When we did see it, it was quite a spectacle and gave us hours of pleasure as we watched the changing colours of the Crystal Bowl developing weird pictures and designs, and satisfying the wishes of the imagination. Its oblong shape and concave patterns caught the sunlight and displayed many pictures, but none was that of the hanging lady.

"'What was more frightening was that the bowl was an heirloom that had been handed down through the generations and I was next in line to become its owner. The thought of owning this mystical bowl was terrifying. What if it did carry a curse as they said? How could I rid it, of its magical powers?

"'As the years passed, the sun continued to shine through the floral curtains and onto the Crystal Bowl, casting shadows of life-like and imaginary pictures that were regularly seen by our marauding visitors. Some were given spooky interpretations that were very scary if told after dark."

'It was always interesting to hear Grandma Maude repeat that legendary tale and she would enjoy telling us these stories just before dark, which would leave us in total fear of what could happen, even though no one in the immediate family had seen the mysterious picture of the hanging lady or spoken of its existence. It also created another problem because Maude's sister Mercy was furious at the way in which visitors had taken over our home, day after day come rain or sunshine, and she was not afraid to speak her mind. Her job was to polish the wooden floor on weekends to a shine that would last through to the following week. That meant a lot of hard work on her hands and keen polishing; she did not take kindly to visitors trailing through the house while she carried out her work. It worse on rainy days when the pathway was muddy; those wet muddy footprints left her beautifully shiny floor looking dull and dirty. Even though she complained, nothing was done because mother was afraid to do anything that might invoke the curse.

'One day, Grandma told us, Mercy decided to get her own back on the visitors and Mercy was left on her own shining the floor. She said, "Mercy had finished her job, and was determined that no one was going to mess up her shiny floor. So, Mercy locked the doors and crept under the bed. It was a place Mercy rarely visited let alone cleaned, but she was determined to save her shiny floor from the visitors' muddy feet. She crawled through the thick dust and found a comfortable spot. It was dark and frightening, but the peace and tranquillity became hypnotic, and was soon sleeping like a baby."

'In a world of dreams, Mercy's peaceful sleep was uninterrupted by disappointed visitors, who, failing to enter the house, turned around and discouraged others from making the journey. She had successfully reduced the visitor's chances of capturing that magical moment when the picture could emerge, and she had saved her beautiful shiny floor from the dirt and grime of those visitor's feet.

'Grandma said that was Mercy's version the one she wanted us to believe because no one could prove differently. Our mother, grandma said, was very pleased to come home to a clean floor that sparkled in shine, and Mercy had the happiest weekend for many years.

'Over the years lots of changes had taken place; after constant handling the beautiful floral curtains began to fade. They had had lost their magic and had to be changed. A generous fruit tree was also growing rapidly outside the window and its branches obscured the sunlight. This fruit tree was bearing its first crop and no one wanted to disturb its growth.

'At the same time, Grandma's sister, my great aunt, became pregnant and the thought of a newborn was just the tonic the family needed to divert their attention away from the hanging lady picture that had consumed their lives. The family was also worried that the

Crystal Bowl had lost its magic and something bad would happen sooner rather than later. Grandma Maude said her mother was the driving force in maintaining the superstition, and was convinced that the Crystal Bowl had magical powers, which made her fearful of her sister's unborn baby. There were talks that the baby's life might become endangered by this unproven curse. This worrying talk made her sister ill, and for a while, she came close to losing her life and the baby's.

'To satisfy their demands Maude's father cut back the branches and allowed more sunlight unto the window. But that was not enough to allow make Crystal Bowl perform convincingly and remove their fears. So they waited for a sign that would give them a clue that the curse had passed. Surprisingly the Crystal Bowl did not show the sign they wanted to see, instead, her sister had gave birth to a baby boy. Whether that was the sign they wanted, no one spoke of it. One thing was sure; the birth brought relief and excitement enough to remove the festering feeling of bad luck. They put their obsessive behaviour aside and welcomed the new life into the world. Grandma said the baby, Ben, was the most beautiful child she had ever seen.

'Baby Ben became the most precious child to have been born in that house. Why? His birth broke the taboo that hung over our families. Even though the craze for the mysterious picture had abated, the arrival of a newborn kept the visitors' interests alive, making the weekends a very happy time to visit the baby.

'Five months later Ben took sick and my great aunt took him to the doctor, who prescribed him some medication and sent him home. Ben came home, was given the medication, and within a few days stopped crying and began to respond to the treatment. Soon the little boy was back to his happy, smiling self and everyone sighed in relief as they thought the clouds of the curse had cleared the horizon. Unfortunately this feelgood factor did not last for long.

'Two days later Ben became sleepy and refused any kind of food; his illness had returned and set tongues wagging. Ben was sleeping for longer spells. The medication had stopped working and Auntie and the families were devastated. The community was ablaze in superstition, their comments aimed at Auntie and the families. The little boy's well-being became their greatest concern and arrangements were quickly made for his return to the doctor.While they got themselves and little Ben ready for the journey, Ben fell asleep and stopped breathing. Although they hurried to get him to the doctor, he died on the way. They were overwhelmed with grief. The news of his death was like a giant tornado, consuming everyone and the gathering crowds wept at the tragic loss of a five months old baby boy.

'Our hearts were gripped in sadness as though we were living the experience and Grandma's cheeks were awash with streaming tears. The story might have taken place many years ago, but its effect was as powerful in her mind. I can imagine, had I been in her position and were Ben my child, the burden of loss would follow me to the end of time, and I, too, would also be overcome with tears and fears.

'The death of Ben, Grandma told us, caused an unpredictable mood of confusion among an already excited group of people in their community. No one wanted to be first to cast doubt on the fascinating prediction the picture might have made, because anyone brave enough to criticise this phenomenon left themselves open to the wrath of the curse. It was easier to accept the story than to have an accident placed at their door, which was made real by Ben's death.

'Grandma Maude went on to say that some months later her mother had to replace the floral curtain, and the fruit tree grew new branches. Worse, they were laden with succulent fruits, which blocked the sunlight. It was a disastrous times for the believers; the Crystal Bowl could not perform and anything could happen. No one noticed the tree was the real cause of their problems.

'The picture had caused a deep and very serious conviction to flourish. People would wish for a particular picture to appear that to them meant some sort of luck. In those days, Grandma said, people believed in anything that seemed convincing enough to change their way of life. Their ideology wasn't based on mystical, astrological and nonsensical ideas that most times only gave idle thoughts room to wander. At last a new curtain was hung up, but it was equally disappointing. Although the colours were the same, it was not as good as the old one. The floral patterns were totally different, making its display unacceptable.

'What was it those people wanted, Grandma wandered? They weren't satisfied that Ben's death could have been the result to the curse and that it was time to let go and move on; it seemed they wanted a disaster of epic proportions to take place. But how much more disastrous did they want it to be, worse than the sudden death of a five months old baby? The mind boggled.

'Age and the weather took their toll and laid claim to the wooden window frame. The sun and rain destroyed the protecting wax and polished surfaces, allowing the water to rot the wood, and leaving it in a state of needy repair. The workmen had to move the table to far side of the room, under another but smaller window. The table had to go somewhere and that was the only space big enough to accommodate it and its precious cargo. The repair of the window was welcome news for Mercy, as it meant no more mopping up of rainwater. However, what came after was an amazing fate that set everyone's eyes ablaze and their hearts beat with joy. At midday, whilst the workmen carried out the repairs, the Crystal Bowl came alive, displaying its magical pictures clear for everyone to marvel at. Sadly, those pictures were of a goat and a bird, no sign of the hanging lady. Grandma said it wasn't what my parents' generation wanted. They were obsessed by this picture of the hanging lady, and any others weren't good enough to satisfy their superstitions. But many families saw any picture as a new revelation that could restore happiness among community and put to rest the enhancing spread of bad luck syndrome.

'By the time grandma had finished telling the story I was the only child still awake. My two brothers, sister and cousin were all asleep leaning on each other. Grandma and I gently lifted them from the floor and helped them into bed, oblivious to the depth in which those mysterious feelings penetrated our great grandparent's lives.

'I have listened to the story several times, said Marybell, 'with all its twists and turns. Yet, I never felt convinced that it was the truth. However, grandma's passion when she told the story left me feeling that she believed it all. And every time this story is told it reminds me that I never asked my brothers and sister what their reaction were to what I termed to be a myth. As children we were terrified of the dark and its magical powers, it wasn't appropriate for children to ask grown-up questions on taboo subjects such as the picture of the hanging lady. But as the years passed and I become an adult, I was still haunted by the authenticity of the story. I was desperate to know the truth and decided to ask my father a few questions, which I hoped would help to allay my fears, even though he wasn't aware of the story.

'I began by asking him if he knew Grandma's home before I was born. He said, "Yes". I was so pleased with his answer so I dived in further. This time the question became jumbled, and he couldn't give me a straight answer. "Stop," he said. "What exactly do you want to know and why?" Well Dad, I said, if you tell me whether or not Grandma had a Crystal Bowl and if a tree used to grow at one of the windows, I will tell you why. Dad confirmed that Grandma did have a Crystal Bowl and a tree did grow outside the window. I was shocked and could not believe my ears. His answer had suddenly smashed my conclusion as to what was claimed as being mysteriously mystical.

'It would appear that my great grandparents and others had failed to realise that picture was a natural reaction, that it was actually generated by the pattern of the floral curtains. And, if anyone or anything were to blame, it would have to be the sunlight and the creative patterns of the floral curtain, because there were no mystical powers in those pictures. While the tree grew and spread its branches, its leaves blocked the penetrating sunlight and changed the pictures of the floral curtains. A simple deduction, I thought, hence the myth or deception of good or bad luck. The question is; did the tree grow before the picture was first seen, and was Ben's birth and death superstitious?'

One thing was certain; Lafty's mother and her Grandma had lived the story several times over and could still hear voices relating the myth. Similar feelings seemed to have affected Lafty's soul. Scary though the story was, children were made to feel peaceful, loved, and safe.

The story had given Lafty time to settle into his new surroundings and reminded him of other times when he had been frightened of the dark. It also highlighted the extent to which adults can pretend to know the mind of a child, when fear dominates their innocence. Lafty's mother believed in what she was doing, convinced it was the best for her son, but in whose eye? Was her decision based purely on her or was it her son? She did not once ask Lafty if he would be happy living with his father, or if he was willing to make friends with a bunch of strangers whose appearance on the open seas at night seemed evil. In one day Lafty had endured more trauma than he had during his twelve years of growth. His mother's decision left him carrying a very high price tag, and drove his brain to think it could become part of his daily routine, which was beyond the scope of a twelve-year-old. It was not the kind of nurturing he had expected.

CHAPTER 8

Friendship

It was time to sleep and allow his young mind to imitate those of his portentous elders by pretending he was asleep and was aboard a ship with glowing lights in all its cabins. His closed eyes invited his thoughts to play with his fears and allow the darkness and the violent action of a displeased ship to remind him of those rocking movements as a baby at bedtime; repeatedly saying, 'Hi-ha mammy, hi-ha daddy,' until his weary body had overpowered his mind and he had lunged into a world of peaceful sleep. His pretence worked, but his rocking and mumbling words kept the vigilant Mud alert. Fear and emotion danced to the tune of the creaking ship and Mud's wondering thoughts. Mud wondered if he would have to reach the edge of madness before he slept. Motionless, he lay awake and waited. He waited and listened for that sudden movement when the crunching noises of that cracking straw-filled mattress gave way to the breathing sounds of a restful child. But by then sleep was no longer an option for Mud, his concern for Lafty's care was growing faster than his brain could control. He wanted to get up and cuddle the lad, but that would be wrong. After all, Lafty was not his son and he could not pretend to be his father. However, the boy's breathing soon became calm and even, relieving the tension that had strangled his body. Thank God, he whispered to himself. Yet, he could not move a muscle. He was fearful that any movement could disturb the little boy's sleep. In silence Mud was soon to realise the discomfort of those mattresses. After all, he was not drunk, his brain was fully alert, and his body had become sensitive to every pinprick of those needle-sharp ends that seemed hell-bent on avenging the many fights and injuries he had inflicted over the years. He felt like a giant pincushion. It took every ounce of self-control to temper the temptation to move. Mud had sacrificed his supper, and his night's sleep to preserve a friendship that had had since childhood.

Ruben was a slick customer who knew how to get the best of everyone he met. Mud, Dusty and Scruffy were particularly susceptible to his schemes. As good as their friendship was, Mud did not put himself out to please Ruben. What Mud did was primarily for Lafty's benefit. Knowing how distressed the boy had been, to see his little body curl up, peacefully asleep, gave him a rewarding sense of achievement, something that his friendship with Ruben had not provided. It was a task he was proud to do. It helped him to look into himself and remind him of the old saying, 'If you can't do a good turn, then don't do a bad one; it might follow you.' That brought home to his brain the caring person he had always been. He could take satisfaction in the fact that Lafty would for the rest of his life remember that night and the care and understanding he was given during his father's absence and the loneliness of the trauma his mother's decision had brought him. Mud could dream of a better tomorrow from the innocence that Lafty represented.

It was only a matter of a couple of hours to the start of Mud's working shift and he became worried that he might have to return to work without sleep, which was probably the longest night he had spent awake, and waiting. He could not avoid thinking of what he believed might be a form of punishment. Maybe it was the reaction to one of his misdeeds and someone or something was having their revenge on him. Lafty's plight had switched on his conscience and set alarm bells ringing about the philanthropy of him and his friends. Those thoughts remind him that he, too, could have been forced to make similar judgements as Marybell and Ruben had on Lafty's future. Mud had always been critical of their actions, and he was not equipped with the true knowledge of her fears or his plans, but he doubted Marybell would have taken her decision lightly. Nor had it been born out of an overnight dream. Her decision, he thought, could have been based on her experience as a child and the culture of her community. And she would have been aware of the implication and long term effects on her son's life, and it was bound to have left her feeling awful. Her fears would have been well-founded, because they had been part of her childhood; the rules of the great plantation by which she was brought up. It was a place where the Master ruled; where families and workers took their orders, regardless of their effect; private, personal or otherwise. Children would be taken from families and put to work. Depending on their physical abilities they would either work at the farm or in the house, and which ever it was no one dared to object because they had no rights. This meant that education was a privileged commodity, given to those the Master selected. He had the power to condition their minds and beliefs, so that they were obedient to his commands at any given time. The Master was the only one who knew what was best for the poor and for the slaves.

Lafty's mother Marybell had grown up in that environment, and was well aware of the treatment of blacks and poor people who were weak and helpless with no representation. There were a few privileged ones who were talented, and their talents were made to fit into the Master's programme. They were also given limited scoop of independence that was far greater than that of Marybell's family. What was ironic was that those privileged few would in many instances become the hustlers of the poor and defenceless. However, they all had one dream that one-day their shackles would be removed and that they would be allowed to become human beings, a dream Lafty mother craved for her son over the years. What she did not understand was how to achieve her ambition.

She realised that someone would suffer but did not imagine it would be her son.

On his occasional visits over the years Ruben had told her stories of opportunities elsewhere and made her more determined to remove her son from what seemed destined. Ruben's stories gave her hope; hope that her son might not become embroiled in the same spiral of slavery she suffered. She wanted the best for her son, to have an education, and to grow up as an upstanding member of the community, enjoying the privileges of the few. Marybell was prepared to go to any length or do anything that would avoid a forceful induction into slavery. And in all honesty she thought Lafty would be grateful for her effort.

Ruben's slippery tongue had given her something to cling onto, the hope of better opportunities elsewhere that would give Lafty the chance to an education and to becoming an independent man, thereby fulfilling her dreams. Those words melted like a smooth flowing river.Marybell had two children, yet there was no emphasis put on her daughter's future. Could it be she was still in love with Ruben, and wanted her son to develop his father's personality? Or was it that sons in those days fetched a higher price when a bride was sought. It was customary for parents to carve their sons' future whether it was in education or in marriage. Moreover, sons were the providers that parents depended on for their old age. So her effort to remove Lafty from becoming a slave boy was, in effect, safeguarding her interests. She might have been illiterate, but she was smart in her thinking. Right or wrong, her decision had placed their friendship at risk and a boy's future in the balance. Mud was right to feel the way he did; he was not privy to Marybell's heart-rending decisions and could only guess from the pain in the little boy's eyes, which could only have come from a mother's deter-mined attitude. How could he in all honesty, refuse her of that one chance that she believed could fulfil the dream she had for her son? Perhaps Ruben could not resist her anguished pleading, Mud thought, knowing that Ruben was partially responsible being Lafty's father. No amount of guessing could settle Mud's mind; he would have to wait until Ruben decided to explain the truth about his plans.

The early morning son shone through the tiny porthole, casting a misty glow of hazy light which lit up the dingy cabin. It was also an alarm clock for the early risers and signalled rest time for the night workers. Having thought deeply about Lafty's situation, the reasons for or against his plight, Mud changed his approach and decided not to confront Ruben head on that morning. Instead, he would allow Ruben the space to explain his plans for Lafty's future. Although Mud's concern was justified, he could not allow any irrational approach to jeopardise years of friendship. He was not equipped with the facts.Mud and the others had been warned of Lafty's appearance and, though they had forgotten, they had made a promise which they were bound to honour, friends or no friends.

Mud's mind had been so busy that he had forgotten the uncomfortable position of his body, but it was time to get up and put those meandering thoughts to rest, even if by doing so it woke Lafty. His father will be back soon, and that should give the boy peace of mind, he thought. Slowly Mud shuffled his massive muscles from what seemed like a child's bed and set his feet firmly on the creaking floor that was littered with pieces of straws from their mattresses. At first glance, the cabin floor was like an overnight horsebox with the groom and jockeys asleep and the horses were no where to be seen. The typical lifestyle of a sailor was far below the standards of a well-groomed racehorse. Poor Lafty, Mud repeatedly told himself, he's not used to these conditions, it's not fair to him. But, what is fair, if you are poor or being treated as a slave, who could you complain to? And, if anyone should demonstrate any sort of kindness or should listen to the cries, what could they do to relieve the burden of being branded – a nobody? Not a lot. Those who tried ended up losing their lives and the lives of others.

Getting clumsily out of bed, Mud's weighty body shook the loose wooden structure, but Lafty was not unduly disturbed and remained in a deep sleep, lapping up a world of unconsciousness. It was reassuring that Lafty remained sleeping, as there was no telling what his unpredictable behaviour could throw up next, and Mud did not have the time to nursemaid a hysterical boy at that hour in the morning. It was okay for Dusty and Scruffy on the opposite side. They were snoring for all their worth, even though it was time for them to get up.

Mud carefully removed the shirt and trousers that had given Lafty such a laugh and neatly folded and placed them on his bed. He then retrieved from the foot of the bed the paint-splattered, greasy, working clothes that looked much the same. Mud finished the delicate task of dressing and quickly gave Dusty and Scruffy a sharp tug, reminding them of the time. He was about to step through the door when Ruben arrived, brandishing one of his usual charming smiles.

'How is my boy?' Ruben asked Mud, hoping to have a glowing and encouraging report, and hearing how wonderful his son was and how pleased they all were at becoming nursemaids on the open seas.

Mud returned a pleasant but casual smile. 'He is a good boy, and we got on well. Ruben, don't you go making too much noise now, he is still sleeping, and we were late getting to bed. Dusty and Scruffy are still sleeping.'

'Lafty is not on his own, so come on, walk with me and talk freely,' said Ruben. His eyes gleamed, anticipating good news. He was hoping that Mud might say he and the others would take full responsibility for Lafty's care. And for a moment a feeling of elation overwhelmed his brain and his heart pounded in excitement. Thank God, he thought, his wishes were about to be fulfilled. That would be brilliant.

Together both men walked away, heading towards Mud's workstation. Arriving there, Mud was more interesting getting on with his work than talking. Ruben had finished his working shift and could spend time talking, but Mud did not have the time to waste in talking; he had his service checks to carry out. Nothing would be left to chance; all working parts and equipment would be checked and double-checked. It was quite feasible for Mud to continue while Ruben followed him around so long as his inspections were being done. This was a practice they had carried out on many occasions. Although they talked about many things, Mud was not talking about the issue that Ruben wanted to hear. It was left out. Why? Ruben was eager to know what Mud had found out about Lafty. And Mud was not in a hurry to share what he had found out. By this time Mud realised Ruben knew very little about his son and decided to play Ruben at his own game. After all Ruben had failed to trust him with whatever plans he had for Lafty's future. It was a secret best kept by Ruben and Marybell.

Mud did not know the reasons why Lafty's mother had given up her son to Ruben, but it became his greatest fear that Ruben might put his son into a plantation house, where freedom was earned, and education an old man's tale. To him, Lafty seemed to have come from a loving, caring home because he was well-built physically and looked fit; strong and capable to work and earn his keep. But working boys lacked opportunities for an education. Mud was struggling to understand the behaviour of his friend. Any loving father, Mud thought, having left his child for eight or more hours with total strangers in a strange environment, would first have a quick look at the child, if only to satisfy his concerns for the child's safety. But that was not Ruben's priority and he failed to meet Mud's estimation of a caring father. Ruben was far more interested in hearing from Mud how he, Ruben, should approach his son. How sad! It was clear from that moment that Lafty's future was in the balance and the gut-wrenching decision his mother had made might turn out to be a useless gesture. Ruben was a father, a fact Mud was sure of, so what made Ruben behave the way he did?

Mud's thoughts were in disarray, and he could only wonder whether Ruben had ever played a fatherly role with his son.

But Lafty was Ruben's responsibility and he and he alone could decide the boy's future, good or bad. So Mud decided to tell Ruben of his experience of Lafty's behaviour during the night. He also told Ruben that he did not get any sleep because the choppy seas had sent the ship dancing to some strange tunes. But that was not exactly what Ruben wanted to hear. He wanted Mud to volunteer all the information he had of Lafty's behaviour that night. What had the boy said? Did he like or dislike the ship and his adventure? Was he missing his mother and his home?

They had been friends all their lives, had strong feelings for each other and knew each other well, but people changed, and Ruben was no exception. He was always inventing a get-rich scheme, and Mud would always be there in support, egging him on, hoping that his dreams would be fulfilled. This time things were different, Mud thought. The future of a little boy was at stake. No matter how much they cared for each other, someone else was involved. It was no longer a mere quest to preserve their friendship but to demon-strate how strong their friendship really was. The memory of Lafty's saddened face helped Mud to try and cement those changes. He was also deeply disturbed at the way in which Ruben had not given their friendship the respect it deserved. He could empathise with Lafty and the plight that had dogged his life, because Lafty could have been one of his children, and that made him more resolute to know what Ruben had planned for the boy. In his quiet and unassuming way, Mud took a radical step and put Lafty's situation on a personal level, as though Lafty was of his own flesh and blood.

Mud's patience was slowly draining away. He felt like child answer-ing a headmaster's questions and became exhausted. Throughout their talks nothing was said to make Ruben any the wiser about his son. Rightly or wrongly, Mud was of the opinion that if Ruben wanted to know more about his child, then he should be prepared to put in the time himself, and be a father. Mud did not think it was his place to tell Ruben of Lafty's fears; the dark, and his refusal to eat, his being sick and unhappy, Mud did not take kindly to Ruben's actions, leaving Lafty with strangers on rusting old bucket for a ship. There was no alternative, in Mud's thoughts. He had made his mind up not to help Ruben know Lafty's likes or dislikes and avoided any further discussion.

Ruben walked away unable to extract the endorsements he had hoped for, which left him none the wiser and his friend with empty feelings.Having worked through the night, tiredness began to arrest his body and sleep became an urgent need. In parting, both men had recognised their responsibility. Even though they were not satisfied, they agreed to continue the discussion later that day or at the end of Mud's shift.But Mud had left Ruben feeling more confused than ever. He was puzzled by his friend's behaviour, which left him with the same question going over and over in his head: Why did I follow Mud? Even then, Ruben could not see that his failure to know his son was the answer. He was out of touch, and his worried brain came close to shutdown. He did not know how to cope with a son he hardly knew, and his friend's behaviour did not help. What had Lafty told Mud, he wondered, to create a sudden change in him? After all, Mud was his best friend. He had not asked him to break the law or to do anything silly on his behalf. He would have done the same for the man. Ruben's mind was in turmoil, though if the truth were told, Mud clearly did not want to become involved in what seemed the unfair treatment of a little boy who could not speak up for himself.

Ruben's rustling feet echoed the alleyways, bringing a sleepy ship to life. He walked at a snail's pace, his thoughts blowing like the wind around his head and, for the first time in all those years, Ruben took notice of his surroundings. He was struck by the penetrating sunlight, as it reached into corners, lighting up the rusts and cracks. He had made that journey on several times and at the same hour of the morning, yet he had failed to appreciate its effect.

Had he been converted? Was he about to suddenly cast aside his selfish attitudes and begin to look at life with an open mind? That might have been the most logical conclusion; this change had come over him far too quickly for there to have been any other explanation. Something had happened during his working hours to modify his attitude. Could it have been a divine intervention?The question was: could it last and for how long? Whatever his plans and motives were, Lafty's presence had sent a massive ripple across everyone's thoughts. The streaming sunlight was a mere reminder of what was plaguing Ruben's mind.

Could there have been another interpretation of what came over Ruben. Could it be attributed to his past, and the fowl deeds he had committed? Were years of neglect and a disturbed conscience catching up with his thinking? Was it the result of the burden of guilt that was bearing heavily on his shoulders? Ruben was the strongest and was most articulate of the gang, but that morning he was stuck for words, and could not think rationally about his plans for Lafty. Mud had been reluctant to support Ruben. He had smashed his expectations. Mud had always supported Ruben ventures, but on that occasion Mud had not been happy to conform to Ruben's wishes, and his decision had brought anguish to Ruben's already confused mind. As Ruben got closer to the cabin door his tendency to change increased, without any read explanation.

Ruben was a practical joker who usually carried out his pranks at the end of his night shift, and that morning was no different. Early morning gave the perfect cover for his jokes to be effective it also provided the opportunity for his favourite jokes to get maximum reaction and send his shipmates scampering from their beds. This would set him up for the day. Ruben would take off his shirt and cap, and carefully hang it over a sweeping brush, holding the brush up above the top of the doorway and allowing the misty sun light to project an image of someone being hanged. Then, to sensationalise his effort, he would imitate the sound of the bosun's voice, shouting as loud as he could, 'Man overboard!' No one would clearly understand what was being said; all they would know was that it was an emergency call. So the frightened sailors would hurriedly scramble from their beds, some half-dressed, others falling over each others trying to get out, and while he would chuckle with laughter, they would fume with anger. But it kept them alert. Some would pick a fight, while others appreciated being woken. And Ruben would always get away with his pranks, because everyone had to attend an emergency call. His humour was tolerated because not all his jokes caused a disruption. Moreover, Ruben infectious smile always won the day.

Ironically, no one noticed the silence that existed after the panic when peace and quiet would flood the cabin and only echoes of the creaking ship dared to break the subdued silence of a passing joker. Unnoticed by his shipmates, which was of little comfort to this man, his thoughts were firmly fixed on the son he wanted to love but he was fearful about how to open up to this lad.

'I don't really know the boy,' Ruben told himself. 'I don't know what he likes or dislikes and, more importantly, what kind of food he likes to eat; what games he plays. All these things I've got to know. He could be stuck aboard this ship for another two to three days, which is not long, but anything could happen to make the journey longer. He is only a child with no experience; I have to work out how I will manage. Like Mud, I too will have to change.'

CHAPTER 9

The Big Change

In thoughtful mood Ruben reached the cabin door. Dusty and Scruffy were awake. Their presence strengthened his confidence, allowing him to feel more relaxed as he made his entry. They were the dependable pair of crutches that he desperately needed. However, he was not the sort of man to allow anyone to become aware of his true feelings. He was a master of disguise, very good at masking his fears and hiding behind the charms and smiles that set him apart from the rest. He greeted his friends with a slap on the shoulder and a massive grin. But all eyes were on Lafty, whose body coiled beneath a rustic coloured covering. These were not the conditions Ruben wanted for his son, but life on a sailing ship was rough and basic.

The long awaited sound of Ruben's voice soon penetrated the little boy's hearing and stimulated his happy nerves. The excitement of his father's presence made his body shake, leaving Dusty and Scruffy to wonder how long he had been awake.

Ruben sat on the edge of the bed, shuddering with nervous tingles, not knowing whether to hug or kiss the contents of the bundle. His body ached, lips dry and tongue too heavy to speak. His outstretched hands reached out to hold his son, wanting to caress his boy, but his shaking fingers rebelled, they were entering uncharted territory. Ruben had not held Lafty for nigh on eight years. They were as strangers. What should have been a free flowing movement, a father holding his son, bringing reassurance and safe feelings,

turned into a bungling presentation of non-committal awkward-
ness. The shame of his action invoked voices in his head which told
him to pull himself together. If Mud could see him then, how
wonderful he would have felt that his friend had finally turned
the page of selfishness, and become a caring, loving father. Lafty
opened his eyes and saw ten years of hope realised; his father was
sitting on the bed beside him, a symbolic part of his dreams. After
a traumatic night, his father's presence made the little boy leapt
from his bundle. His face awash with one of the most beautiful of
smiles, and arms apart, he hugged his father. There was no shame,
no embarrassment and no delay. It was a show of sheer love and
happiness. He did not have to say anything. His hero was there. He
felt safe again and that was all that mattered in the little boy's mind.
The time was right for bonding to commence. Father and son locked
in embrace, occasionally looking at each other, wondering who
loved who most. Their silent thoughts had made the connection
that was far long overdue. But Ruben's thoughts were plagued with
ill feelings about his plans for Lafty. What if they failed to mater-
ialise, he asked himself? If it went wrong, he could not live with
himself. Ruben seemed to have turned a new page in his life, and
began to see his son in a different light. His son was no longer a
pawn in his chess game. Lafty was his son, from whom a megaton
of love and affection was cascading towards him. Whatever his
plans were, they would have to be changed, he thought. And, at
that moment, as though Lafty was reading his father's thoughts,
tears of joy trickled from his cheeks and created a damp patch on
his father's shoulder. Only a man without a heart could divert from
a mother's wishes for her child, the wishes she had for her son. Man
and boy tightly held each other, and allowed the heat from the
morning sun, the blustering wind and the lashing waves to drive
the ship forward on to their destination. In the meantime their
thoughts set them adrift, to meander through life, realising they
were no longer alone. Wading through the future, Ruben realised

his middle age had slowly dawned. Soon he would have to give up sailing. His past was fast catching up with him. Living a sailor's lifestyle was becoming more and more disruptive, making it too strenuous to keep up with his growing children. Moreover, his wife needed his presence. It was time, he thought, to get to know his family better and enforce the discipline that was needed in the home. He did not really know those children as a father should. Ruben was thinking along the same lines as his friend Mud and found himself torn between carrying out his selfish plans and the nagging thoughts of being a good father, fulfilling the promise he had made to Lafty's mother. If he had not been confused at any other time, he was then. The more he thought of what he ought to do in his son's best interest, the more infected his mind became to the consequences of his actions. Ruben could not make up his mind knowing that his plans could put Lafty's future at risk. Not only did he have to take the consequences seriously, he also had to take into consideration the valued friendships of Mud, Dusty and Scruffy. After all, he had already pushed their loyalty to its limit. Earlier, Mud had demonstrated his unwillingness to co-operate with his ideas and Dusty and Scruffy would follow Mud's lead, which could leave him with no plans or friends – a scary prospect.

As he sat and basked in the elation of his son's greeting, his wondering mind gently subsided. Suddenly it dawned on him that the ship was silent, as though it was listening to his thoughts with grave disapproval. Dusty and Scruffy had made their contributions; they quickly dressed and left the cabin, leaving it to play host to a worried father and celebrating son. In its stillness, father and son's hearts beat as one, changing the course of all their plans. From that moment, Ruben would not be forgiven if he should put Lafty's future at risk. Compelling thoughts filled his head, urging him to do what was right for his son, fulfilling the wishes of the woman he once loved.

When Ruben had agreed to take Lafty away from his mother, it had not occurred to him that he would have to carry out any soul-searching about his motives. He could not think rationally, nor could his brain make any positive decisions. A man who always had all the answers, he was suddenly found wanting. He needed help and fast.

Ruben needed to understand why he had made the commitment to Lafty's mother, and how positive his plans were. Would they achieve the results he had prayed for; fulfilling the promises he had made Marybell? Firmly pressed against him, the warmth that radiated through their closeness made him reflect on the boy as just a child, further complicating his thoughts. It was easy to recall as the boy had grown up, how proud his mother was of him; more so on days when the boy came home from playing, and told her that he had fought others who had teased him about his absent father. Both father and son seemed to have developed similar patterns of thinking.

Lafty looked into his father's eyes and said, in his own way, 'My friends teased me and it hurts. They said bad things about you.'

Ruben's heart melted in sorrow, but he could not change the past, even though Lafty's future tortured his soul. Those had been hurtful times for Lafty, but he did not care to recall them. All that mattered then was being with his father. And, for a moment he could forgive his mother. Even though he had only been away from her one day and night he carried hate in his heart for the mother he loved. The trauma of that night pushed him to think he would never want to see her again. He was too young to understand his mother's reasons for the actions she took. Lafty was no different from any other young boy who wanted to imitate the adventures of his father, even though the reality could be devastating.

He did not want to leave home, but equally he wanted to live with his father, and being with him then signalled the beginning of their life together. His mother had told him of his aunt, Ruben's sister, whose home would become his new home. But he was a child and could not comprehend the complicity of the situation. He could not grasp the difference in his father's living accommodations. The little boy was of the opinion that his father and aunt's arrangement was similar to that of his mother and their family. Living with his father, Lafty thought, could wipe away all the pain, fear and sadness he had endured since he came aboard.

The sight of a father and son locked in silence, their thoughts ablaze and no one rushing to put out the flames, was rewarding. But time was ticking away; Ruben's erratic heartbeat slowly regained its composure. Verbal communication was as important and it was Ruben's responsibility to open up and commence some sort of dialogue.

'Did you sleep well last night?' Ruben asked. Lafty smiled and nodded his head. 'I told you my friends would make you comfortable.' If only he had known how Lafty had felt throughout that night.

'Yes sir.'

'Have you eaten? You must be hungry; I'll go and get you something to eat as soon as the kitchen is open.'

'Thank you, sir,' the boy answered in a muffled sound.

'I have to go to work tonight, so after you have eaten I must get some sleep. But I will show you where you can and cannot go, and there are two cabin boys on board you might like to make friends with. They are not a bad set of boys, but I must tell you I will not have any blasphemy or bad language. Do you know what I mean?'

'Yes sir,' answered Lafty, nodding his head.

The boy was dumbstruck. It was the first his father had spoken so many words to him but, worse, he had spoken with a rebuking attitude that was bad enough to frighten a grown man, let alone a child.

Ruben's concerned mind was playing tricks on his macho ego; the need to make a conquest had landed him a son, whom he had treated as someone else's child. But the game was over for him and his responsibility was there to remind him of it. He could not take

Lafty back to his mother, so he had to get his plans sorted. Having told Lafty they were going to the kitchen, his defensive nerves spun into action and tightened his grip.

This behaviour could only suggest what was going on in the boy's mind. If he should loosen his grip, he might not see his father again. Their bodies clamped even tighter, and summoned the vibrating echoes of Lafty's pounding heart, like a jackhammer against Ruben's body.

Still, Ruben had two days in which to perfect his plans, or find a plausible excuse to send Lafty back to his mother. But that was not the outcome either Lafty or his mother wanted. Neither would relish that result. Lafty's dream was to live with his father, and his mother would do anything to avoid her son being sent into slavery. She wanted him to have an education, which was more than what she had had. Surprisingly, they both wanted the same for Lafty. The trouble was that Ruben had never before tested his feelings for his son and was unaware of the tremendous love he had for him. Only then he realised how important a father's love was to his son. But there was very little Ruben could change at that late hour, given the complicity of the situation. Any action he took would cost more than its worth to redress the imbalance his absence had created.

The combination of a frightened boy and a worried father was a recipe for a level of uncertainty that might have devastated the development of any long-term relationship. A battle had begun in Ruben's head as the past collided with the present with no solution in sight. More urgent in his mind were the conditions he had imposed on Lafty. He was well aware of Lafty's poor home life; yet his mother had taken pride in keeping his children and her home together. She would not appreciate knowing that her son was sleeping on this uncomfortable straw mattress with its fall-outs littering the floor, in a cabin overcrowded with total strangers. Ruben's sudden conversion had made him more thoughtful of Lafty's mother's concerns. There was a spark of love in his eyes, and if he played his cards right those feelings could be kept alive. However, if she knew that her son was unhappy and it was his fault, it could put an end to any thought of togetherness. Maybe that was the driving the force that had forged the change. He loved the way in which she had brought up his son. Mind you, he would not have expected less. She lived a respectable lifestyle, which made it easy for her children to grow up and adopt good principles. But what was going on in Ruben's head? Had he become a saint overnight?

If Lafty was Ruben's only son it could give him a reason to pre-serve his genes. But what else was causing such irrational thinking? His half-baked scheme was about to backfire. He also owed his friends an explanation as to his actions and was yet to show grati-tude for their help. Ruben also needed a credible story to tell Lafty, enough to convince the boy that his best interests were his father's priority. But caressing the feel of Lafty's soft, smooth skin against his tough rustic body was a first time experience that begun to melt those bulging muscles, and ignite feelings of fatherly love. Ruben knew then that he had to tell his son the truth and reject any selfish thoughts.

He should courageously suggest that the boy should know that he was not coming home to live with him. The truth had to be told, he thought, but how? The boy might plunge into a fit of depression, then what would he do? There was no easy answer and the reality of Lafty's future remained unsolved. If Lafty were removed from Ruben's plans, where would Ruben put the boy and with whom? Ruben knew that he could not take Lafty to his home. Any such act could put his marriage in jeopardy and probably split the family. Those plans have been circulating his head for a long time and a result was close, so close he could taste it. But to succeed meant Lafty could end up becoming a slave child, despite his mother's expressed wishes. Ruben could not think straight. His soul was on fire, torched by Hell's fury. But he could not make a decision that might destroy his son's future and end any happiness for his mother.

There was no other choice but to let nature take its course, hoping that a better solution could be found in the passing days.

Ruben's friends knew that whatever his plans were, he had placed a great deal of trust in them and he became sad for him. But it was becoming clear to them that those plans were more like a misadventure. Lafty had a particular function to fulfil which was instrumental in making his dream a reality. Suddenly, an air of uncertainty changed his behaviour. But, why?

The noisy pulley-wheels and sliding ropes of the rigging reminded the little boy of a bird he had found the day before he had been taken from his home. He wondered if that bird had lived or died. However, being there with his father, holding hands, made him feel like a king with his victorious army marching into the town square, lapping up the elation of a celebrating crowd. His tiny finger sank deep into his father's muscular hand as they gingerly made their way to the kitchen. If Mud could have seen them, how gratified he would feel. Aglow in happiness, sailors hailed their respect to Ruben and his son. It was reassuring for the little boy. Ruben thought all this adoration could redeem his son from a bad situation. Those voices and their comments were very different from the leg pulling stunts of his sailor friends. He was a father who was about to be propelled into a better future. Could their assertion be right, he wondered? Only time would tell.

Soon their happy faces arrived at the door of the kitchen, a small enclosure with its main feature a large iron cooking pot, seated precariously on what was described by many as a stove. Burning wood fuel, the fire sparked brightly beneath the boiling pot, filling the air with a smell that was not so encouraging to the boy's stomach. He had encountered nasty smells in the pass, but it did not affect his stomach as badly as the rolling ship. Haunted by the previous day's experience, he also knew that complaining would spoil the embracing relationship they formed. Instead, his eyes quickly scanned the surroundings hoping to find something to remind him of home. But what he saw made him scared. A wooden bench secured to the wall had just enough room to seat three people, yet five giant-sized men were sat there. Watching grown men being tossed about like toys on an open shelf was a funny sight for the little boy's eyes.

As he sat and waited with his father, the developing patterns of the day emerged and soon the gangways were filled with colourful language, while the blustering wind filled the giant sails and sent the ship rolling like a playful kitten. The fresh morning breeze had blown the overnight thoughts clear from Ruben's head and left him to focus on Lafty's happiness.

'Right Lafty, it's time I got you something to eat and you must have a good wash after.' Ruben had cast from his mind the fact he had not slept, which would have appeared strange to those that knew his character. The hot food slid from side to side on the cook's table making the boy nervous and forcing him to hold on to his father for dear life, further boosting his confidence. More importantly they became the centre of attention, turning his father into some kind of hero. While deep inside the boy quavered at the inexperience of the father he needed, he knew his prayers had been finally answered.

Ruben's mug was as chipped as his friend's mug and looked just the same. The cook filled it with a rustic looking liquid, which could have been coffee, and a piece of bread as hard as a brick, with tiny holes for ventilation. Each sailor was equipped with their own mugs and other conveniences, something Ruben had overlooked. Lafty would have to share his father's. But Lafty did not mind. In fact he was excited to drink from the same mug as his father, because that was part of his dreams. As for all the chips, if the mug was good enough for his father, then it was good enough for him. And for a moment they became two men sharing the same drink. He was no longer a twelve-year-old boy, but Lafty, son of Ruben. And he was sitting beside the man he had lived for. Neither the foul-tasting drink nor the feeble, infested cornbread was of any importance, his father's presence was worthy of all the tears and pains he felt. Drinking from his father's mug evoked memories of his so-called friend's teasing, 'You haven't got a father.' They were wrong, he thought, and those wonderful words of adventure spoken by his mother's lips had become a reassuring cushion as the reality unfolded.

A new day had dawned in Ruben's life and the things he once taken for granted were suddenly blooming with a fresh and innovating sense of achievement, something he was not quite prepared for at that early stage. Lafty's presence had exposed a part of Ruben's character that had never been seen by anyone, including himself. His face shone brightly, lighting up the joys of a happy man and delighted father. Ruben finally had news to share with his loyal friends, Mud, Dusty and Scruffy; news they would be pleased to hear, especially that of their friend Ruben's conversion. Mud, more than the others, would be extremely pleased at Ruben's decision, knowing that Lafty might yet have the kind home his mother had wished for him. They could also feel proud that they had played a big role in caring for this little boy who had become their adopted son. And, whether or not his future disrupted Ruben's plans, it would not be a bad thing because no harm would come to him. But they would be sad that they had not witnessed the moment when Ruben had given in to his responsibility and had to come clean to his son Lafty.

For the first time Ruben was pleased he was not sharing that moment of bravery with his trusted friends, but with the son to whom he owed much explanation. The truth, my son, he told himself, will be told, but for now let us enjoy these wonderful moments and live as we should have done, all those years.

That day Ruben began a new life with his son, in the hope that he could solve the problem, within the next three to four days, of where and with whom Lafty would spend the rest of life. He even thought of asking his best friend Mud if he might help, if all others failed. But how could he ask Mud, he wondered, when Mud was already closely involved?

CHAPTER 10

The Storm

Three days had passed during which the four men had settled their differences. Ruben had explained his desire to have Lafty close to him, but that he could not take the boy into his home, nor could he take him directly to his sister, without handing him over as a slave child. They had all agreed that that was not the right answer, but no one had come up with a better solution to his dilemma. But on that third evening, while Ruben went to work his shift, Dusty and Scruffy were having a wash, and Mud and Lafty went to have their evening meal, an amazing change took place.

They arrived on deck enjoying the stiff but freshening breeze which was common in the Caribbean Sea. No one took it seriously. Its strength was not alarming, though the sailors busied themselves securing everything on the deck. But as fast as the sailors could secure the ship the wind got stronger, whipping up mighty swells that began to dwarf the ship, violently tossing it in all directions. They thought they had to hold onto what they could, and hope the storm would pass as quickly as it started.

Waves as tall as mountains began to flood the ship at an alarming rate, while the blustering wind gathered strength, ripping the giant sails to pieces. Some blew away; others were left flapping in the wind. Then the main mast broke into several pieces; some landed on the deck, others washed overboard. One piece missed Lafty's head by inches, which frightened Mud more than Lafty. Mud quickly tied a safety line around Lafty's waist and anchored it to the broken mast, but as he did a section of the wooden structure was carried in the wind and landed on Mud, sending him crashing to the deck followed by a massive wave that swallowed the ship.

Man and boy both scrambled for help. Mud was pinned to the deck and seemed badly hurt. Sprawling overboard, and being pulled by the strong current and the wooden plank deeper into the surging water, the frightened little boy fought to untie the knot, thinking his end had arrived. Mud was nowhere to be seen. Lafty was swallowing water and could hardly breathe and his strength was no match for a raging sea. Worse, everything was pitch-black in darkness. He had no idea how close he was to the ship, or where Mud or his father were. He could hear the ship breaking up like twigs snapping into pieces while the clouds above poured out every drop of the rain they carried. Drowning though he was, his father became his greatest concern. He could remember him going to work in the engine room but worried desperately about where he was and whether he had managed to get out. Desperate to help Mud, Lafty screamed for his father, Dusty and Scruffy, but all in vain. The only answer was the thundering blast of the sea.

The thought of losing the father he had waited so long to embrace was more than he could bear. His ears were filled with water and he could not hear any recognisable sounds, nor could he breathe. His tortured soul cried out, 'Why me? Why me?' but there was no one there to give an answer. What was actually only a miserable few minutes seemed a lifetime of slow death. The little boy tried to swim to the surface but the waves were rising higher than his strength could take him, and he was losing the will to fight. The mighty waves tossed him like a rag doll. They too strong for him, and he lost consciousness. But by then his wooden anchor had surfaced and kept his body afloat. If he had been conscious, he could have seen the devastation was going on around him.

Whether it was by chance, luck, or destiny, Lafty was not drowned. The broken mast to which Mud had tied him kept him safe. How could a boy have survived a storm of such ferocity when seasonally experienced grown men had failed to be as fortunate? Could a greater power, such as God's, have been at work? If so, why had God not turned away the storm, knowing that a boy would be terrorised? Even a credible answer would not have made Lafty any more grateful when he discovered the seriousness of his experience. Lafty had found the same God very helpful.

The little boy was set adrift, left to the mercy of an unforgiving sea for eight hours with no knowledge of where he was, what or who was taking care to make sure he was safe. It was not until the early hours of the following morning that he opened his eyes and saw the beauty of a shining sun and the elegance of clear blue sky, with no signs of a storm. His frightened brain hastened his legs to stand and, only then, he realised he had been precariously perched on a plank of wood. As he tried to stand, he fell into the water, screaming for his mother. After a fight to regain his position on the plank, he looked around and was mesmerised by the sight of miles and miles of water stretching towards the skyline. What am I doing here, he wondered, hoping that someone would come to his rescue. The panic button was well and truly pressed. He thought he might as well die. No one was going to find him, other than the razor sharp teeth of the killer sharks. 'I don't want to be eaten by a shark,' he cried out.

Try though he might to remember what had happened before he opened his eyes, he could not. His brain was in utter confusion, nothing seemed to fit and there was no explanation to what had happened, when, or where. The burning sun became his friend and began to caress the little boy with its hot smiling beams, drying up his uncovered skin and parching it to a pale grey colour, which was of no comfort. He was thirsty, and while streaming tears washed the salt from his bruised face, memories slowly filtered back. The lapping water filled his mouth, but it did not slake his thirst. He wondered where his father was, where Mud was. Maybe they were still on the ship, he thought. So why were they not looking for him? He was hungry, tired and thirsty, and suffering the after-effects of a storm-battered night.

'Where are they now?' he asked himself. 'Just as I thought; they are all the same as my mother. She gave me away, the same way they have left me here to die. Please, someone help me to get on dry land.'

The calm sea was very kind, and a cool breeze refreshed his hot and thirsting body. Lafty laid down on the plank, his hands and feet dangling in the water, with only the whooshing sounds of crashing waves in the distance to engage his thoughts. Did he want to give up and die? The answer was no.

'I want to live' he cried, 'and go home with my father, even with Mud if my father is not around.'

He had spent three wonderful days with his father during which Ruben, having come to terms with his responsibility, had promised the boy a very enjoyable time which he was looking forward to. However, while he lay on the broken mast, bobbing up and down on the swells, the powerful current was gently taking him and the plank closer to the beach. He could only see a short distance ahead but the water whooshing against his floating carriage became a strange noise coming from the sea. It was so scary that he wet himself. Having to stay still in fear of falling made it worse. Could this be the shark that was going to eat him, he wondered. He could also hear what might have been the voice of a human person in the distance over his right shoulder, but dismissed the possibility that anyone would be anywhere near. At a point short of hysteria he could see mountains of water quietly moving towards him. His body froze in fear, so much so that he began to pray, 'Our Father who art in Heaven', certain that when that mountain of water reached him, there was no chance of him surviving. The plank began to wobble, rising higher and higher as it climbed the mountain of water. 'Any minute now,' he thought, 'I'll be thrown off and this time I'll probably drown, or the sharks will have their long-awaited meal.'

Once again he could hear that noise, louder, and with it came a crackling sound as though someone was chewing ice. This was even more frightening. Summoning all the courage he had, he lifted his head and twisted his body into the direction from the noise was coming. This allowed him to see far into the distance to the welcome sight of a fisherman's boat coming towards him. He was happy, sad and frightened and the echoing voice kept on saying, 'Can you hear me, lad?' Lafty tried to lift his hand but became unsteady. Disturbed by the swell from the fisherman's boat, he lost his balance and toppled from his perch. The frightened fisherman hurried towards him, grabbed his flapping body and pulled him into his boat. He then untied the knot and hauled the plank aboard his tiny boat, making safe the little boy and his carriage.

Relieved and thirsty, Lafty's smiling face radiated a kind, happy feeling that was rarely seen. The storm had left the little boy ragged with cuts and bruises that had been washed clean by the salted sea water.

The happy smiling fisherman said, 'My name is Griff, what is yours?'

Lafty smiled and made an odd sound that was frightening to the fisherman. This led him to believe that the boy was far worse than he had suspected. There was visible swelling and grazing around the boy's body which had probably been caused by the wet rope and gave rise to the fisherman's suspicions that the boy could also be suffering from one or more broken ribs. Griff tried to comfort Lafty, aware that the boy was in pain. He offered him a drink of fresh water, which Lafty thought was the greatest gift he had had in many years. Lafty drank the water and smiled, allowing his parting lips to mumble, 'Thank you, sir.'

'Thank God for that,' said the fisherman. 'He can talk.' It was a pity Griff did not know that was the limitation to Lafty's speech.

Pointing out the direction to his home, Griff tried to strike a conversation with the lad, saying, 'Over there is where I live, about two miles away.'

Though Lafty was in pain he never stopped smiling. Maybe he was too excited that someone had come and saved him from the shark's razor-sharp teeth or from drowning. He only hoped that his father and Mud were waiting ashore to take him home when he arrived. Thinking the way he did was proof that he was unequipped to comprehend the seriousness of his predicament, how fortunate it had been for him. Griff headed his boat towards home and began to row as hard as he could, happy in the knowledge that he had made the biggest catch of all, something that money could buy. But Griff could not get Lafty to say another word, he just smiled, which made Griff anxious and made him question the way he had spoken to the boy. Maybe the lad could not understand what he had been saying, he thought. Still, he kept on talking, hoping it would build the boy's confidence, relax his troubled mind and restore shattered nerves.

Griff was right; Lafty was in pain that was getting more demanding than the thought of trusting another stranger. It seemed to be the only thing he had been doing over the past few days, and look where it got him. First he had trusted his father, then Mud, and now Griff. How much more trusting would he have to do, he wondered. In the boat next to Lafty was a heavily wrapped parcel, which Griff gently unwrapped. From the parcel he gave Lafty two homemade biscuits. They were dry to chew but it was very encouraging to see Lafty make a meal of it. Lafty was hungry and had learnt to accept food from strangers since he had joined the ship. Griff the fisherman began to row his boat with an extra pull in every movement of the oars.

Aged about fifty, Griff had been a sailor for many years, but had had to give up travelling to be near his sick wife. During his working years his journeys had taken him to most islands in the

Caribbean waters, where he had had similar experience of sudden storms that sometimes left a trail of devastation. He could empathise with Lafty's plight. However, he never gave up taking his boat out to fish. Most days he would be up at the break of dawn to catch the food he loved. Lobster was his favourite and he would often row out to sea on his own to a special spot about two miles from shore, where he found the best breeding ground for lobsters. His wife also loved the succulent taste of the shell fish which gave him extra pleasure in making the journey as often as he could. Every two days or so Griff would row out and collect his catch. But that morning he did not get the chance. Lafty was a much more rewarding catch. The little boat calmly rode the waves as though it was rejoicing at the good news. Griff had two loves in his life, the little boat and his wife. They were the most precious things in the world to him and he loved them equally. Like a cat or a dog the boat seemed to jump to his commands. He would talk to it and would expect an answer even if it was a mere wobble. Griff introduced Lafty to Nelly the boat saying, 'This little man is going to be our friend. Say hello to him.'

Griff wobbled the boat as if to say, 'Okay,' which Lafty thought was funny. Griff turned to Lafty and said, 'And how are you feeling, little fellow?' Lafty nodded that he was okay. 'That is good. It won't be long now, only another hour and we'll ashore.'

In the distance the sun began break the mist and light up the rising peaks of some mountains and this brought a wider smile to Lafty's saddened face. 'Very soon,' he thought, 'I'll see my father and Mud, then I will thank Griff and will not forget what he has done today.'

Griff saw Lafty was in deep thought and appeared lost. He said, 'I can't keep calling you little man, so what is your name?' The little smile said nothing.

They had been together for nearly two hours now, in which time Lafty spoke three words. 'This lad is hurting a lot more than he wanted to say', Griff told himself. 'You can see the hurt in his eyes.' And then out loud he said, 'Okay lad, say no more leave it until we get home.'

Lafty did not know that Griff meant with regard to home, that neither Ruben nor Mud would be there waiting. The boat was getting closer and closer to land as the shape of small buildings along the shoreline came into view and this set his heart racing with excitement. He wanted to laugh and shout for his father but his swollen side became painful. He thought perhaps he had twisted it when he had tried to look for the shoreline.

It was strange, he thought, how calm the sea seemed that morning. It was the calmest it had been since they had set sail four days ago. A few hundred yards and the sea thickened with a flotilla of small boats, some in readiness to sail, some returning from a night of fishing, while others just danced to the movements of a delighted sea.

Griff shouted to his friend, Desney, 'Has anyone washed ashore?'

'No Griff', came the reply.

'Ask around', he said. 'Find out, Desney, if anyone has seen or picked up anything that could have come from a shipwreck. Ask if they've heard of any shipwreck or a violent storm during the night.'

'One sailor says there were high winds on the north coast but not enough to cause damage.'

Griff became puzzled as he tried to make sense of Lafty's appearance and wanted an answer. It was clear that the boy was tied to the plank which was a section of a ship's mast but he had said nothing that could give him a clue as to what had happened. He began to wander if someone had thrown the boy overboard and wanted it to look like a shipwreck. Nothing seemed to fit. Lafty's discovery seemed very suspicious.

The message quickly reached his friends, and other sailors, that something was not quite right, and that their help was needed. They came thick and fast knowing that it was too early for his return. They could not work out what had gone wrong if anything. After all, he was standing in the boat and seemed well. But what they did not know was that Lafty was lying in the boat.

The ragged little boy sat in the middle of the boat and his pitiful waterlogged face told a story that no one was in a hurry to hear. Their many hands dragged the boat onto the sand and onto a safe mooring. But Lafty was too ragged to leave the boat; it was left to Griff's friend Desney to hurriedly fetch some clothing to preserve the little boy's modesty.

It was a moment of sheer joy both for Lafty and Griff; they were safe from the perils of the mighty sea. And for once Griff could breathe a sigh of relief knowing that the boy was alive. His achievement had surpassed anything he could have ever dreamt. He was not the only elated person on the shore that morning. In fact everyone around the boat was showing their delight at what was seen as a miracle. However, it was also terrifying; everyone that came to the boat wanted to lend a helping hand, which was much too much for a very fragile little boy. The shore was set alight with excitement as friends and neighbours and friends clambered to see this little boy.

While they waited for Desney to return, Lafty raised his head above the edge of a rocking boat and looked as far as he could, hoping to spot his father or Mud among the crowd. It was then more than ever that he needed their presence. But wherever he looked he could not recognised either of their faces. His puffed eyes watered and nose was as wet as a puppy dog's. Who were these people and where was he? His wandering thoughts could not console his frightened brain.

'I want my mother,' he cried out as his weakened heart skipped a beat. 'Am I going to die?' It was a statement his helpless brain could not justify.

Desney arrived with a shirt and trousers belonging to his son. 'You can keep them until you get your own.' Griff took the clothes and with Desney's help they gently dressed Lafty.

With a half-hearted smile Griff held his hands. 'Come, little man, we are going home. We have had enough for one day. We need to wash this dried salt from your skin and get your cuts and bruises dressed. A hot cup of soup and a good night's sleep should make you as right as rain. Say no more, we are going home.'

CHAPTER 11

Miracle Boy

Griff friend's Desney, a very big fellow, had been born and brought up in their little fishing village and they had been friends for many years. Usually they would have gone fishing together, but that morning Desney had to carry out repairs to his boat, leaving Griff to fish on his own. Nevertheless, Desney was there when it really mattered. Desney lifted Lafty from the boat like a rag doll and headed for Griff's house, followed by a crowd of anxious people surprised and puzzled at the child's appearance. No one knew what to make of it. Lafty was a stranger who did not have the features of anyone they knew on the island. Thank goodness that it had happened early in the morning when the villagers were half asleep and only the fishermen and women were on the beach.

Desney's huge muscles reminded Lafty of his father and set him off crying. He could take comfort that his father's muscles were bigger and a lot gentler against his body. Ruben's muscles did not hurt as Desney's did. His hands were pressing against his bruised ribs and made him very uncomfortable. He was clearly in pain but did not and could tell anyone. He was too scared to complain. Furthermore, they might not understand what he was trying to say. With the number of conversations that were going on around him it would be difficult for them to hear.

Arriving at the house, Desney took Lafty through the opening held by Griff and inside, sitting him on a chair. His grip on Lafty was as such that Lafty did not see anything of the journey other than a brightening blue sky. The commotion in and outside the house woke Griff's wife, Mrs Farkinson, who came out to see what the noise was about and found a pitiful looking boy who was in need of immediate care. There was no need for a light. The sun had plenty to give and, as though it knew of the joy that had existed within the home, it shone brighter, lighting up every crack and opening in the house. She walked over to Lafty, expressing a loving, caring smile and said, 'Hello lad, and what is your name?'

Her smiling face reminded him of his mother, and in a way it reduced the tension of being in these strange surroundings. Mrs Farkinson did not wait for his answer but continued to check Lafty over for any signs of broken bones, and assess how many injuries he sustained. 'Griff,' she said, 'light the fire and boil some water. This lad needs a warm cup of tea and something to eat. Thank you, gentlemen, you can come back later and see how he is.'

Griff also thanked his friends and promised to keep them informed of any developments. Off the men went to continue what they were doing, whether it was selling their night catch, or just setting out to fish. Griff and his wife were left with the little boy to nurse him back to health. The men went away as puzzled as they had come.

Everyone thought Lafty's appearance was miraculous and became excited at the wondrous happening that had taken over their little sleepy village. One of the men shouted, 'This could become a place of pilgrimage. After all, nothing so unusual has ever happened in the country, let alone in our village.' Others ran through the village waking those that were asleep, telling them that a miracle had happened. 'A little boy was found alive, floating in the sea,' they said. The news began to spread like wild fire through and beyond the village and it was not long before gathering crowds discussed what no one could figure out.

Mrs Farkinson had been a teacher at the missionary school for many years, but had had to give up when she had hurt her back and had found it too painful to walk or concentrate on teaching. Unable to do much for herself, her husband Griff had had to give up his job as a sailor and take care of his wife. However, she had begun to feel better over the passing weeks and had decided to teach the children of her church at Sunday school lessons until she was fully enough recovered to resume teaching at the missionary school. Regardless of the pain she suffered she was alert. Having been working with children throughout her adult life she was adequately equipped to deal with Lafty's needs. She was in her early 50s and but had had no children, though it had been an ambition they had longed to fulfil. Looking at Lafty knowing the circumstance in which he was brought to her, it seem logical that this little boy was indeed the miracle they had been praying for. She began to selfishly hope that Lafty would remain in her care for as long as it was possible, even to the end of her life.

Having checked the boy's injuries, and still waiting for him to tell her his name, a process she had gone through several times, Mrs Farkinson decided to give little boy her own name until he objected or else told her his real name. 'Now little man,' she said. 'Until you say differently I have to call you something, so how about if I call you Sabuer? Would you mind?' she asked.

Lafty's eyes popped open to with a surprising glare, wondering when his father would arrive and put a stop to this naming. He did not mind the name, but was afraid that his father might miss him, because he would be asking for Lafty and not Sabuer, which was the wrong name. This caused him more anguish than the physical pain of his cuts and bruises. Griff entered the room carrying the warm water and halted Lafty's train of thoughts. The water was in a white enamel basin which looked similar to the one he had seen at the plantation house and he thought these people had to be very rich. Griff's presence was the help Mrs Farkinson needed to remove the boy's clothing and expose his badly bruised side and cut legs which, thank God, were not life-threatening. Her only concern was the swelling that appeared around his waist, suggesting he could have broken a rib or two.

They washed the salt from the little boy's body then dressed the cuts and tightly bandaged his ribs to stop him twisting and hurting. As soon as they had finished some neighbours arrived on the doorstep, having heard the news, and offered their help. It was a pleasing moment for the Farkinsons as they watched their friends run around finding something to do. Some went to fetch porridge, while others went to get fish for cooking. It was their belief that the boy was hungry for a healthy meal. These ladies worked fast and efficiently and in a short time they had prepared a meal the hungry lad was happy to eat. The drink and biscuit Griff had given him earlier that morning was the only food to have passed his lips in ten hours. Lafty was very grateful to the ladies and the Farkinsons. They had washed him, dressed him and made him comfortable; what more could he expect? He was a child away from home for the first time, who had been saved by the broken mast and a Good Samaritan from a fate worse than death. His memory of his ordeal was somewhat hazy and he was desperate to know what had happened to his father, but could not communicate his thoughts to Griff or Mrs Farkinson. Even though they had demonstrated that were good people, they were also strangers, which made him afraid of their intentions. Could they have been the monsters he had dreamed about in his sleep?

He looked their home, which was bigger than the home his family shared. They had a beautiful wash basin, chairs, a table, lots of decorations, pictures, drinking glasses, cups and plates – almost everything the same as the great house, though the master was a slave-driver and was not very nice. These people could have been slave masters, after all they were rich. His only comfort came from the fact that Griff was a sailor like his father, and rich people did not go fishing alone in a small boat. Lafty did not know what to make of his situation but hoped that his father would come and get him soon. There was no pain, only discomfort that he could handle if stayed still. The porridge was tasty but not as sweet as his mother's.

Up until then, Lafty had not uttered a word. Though Mrs Farkinson and her neighbour, Mrs Fagan, made a fuss of him, he remained speechless, which was worrying to those ladies who wanted to see him happy. However, their motherly love and attention relaxed his mind and sent his tired body to sleep.

Sad though Lafty's situation was, Mrs Farkinson was a very happy lady. At last she had someone other than Griff to talk to, more so a child as Sabuer who until further explanation would remain in her care. Griff realised what she was thinking and went from the house to explain his nervous anticipation to his friends and to make some kind judgement on the boy's appearance. As he made his way to the beach hut where the gathering men searched for an answer, a boat arrived from the neighbouring island carrying news of a shipwreck some fifty miles away. There had been no survivors. This was great news for the Farkinsons, but would be bad news for Lafty when he was told. The village court was in session with each man endorsing and congratulating Griff's catch. It was the blessing he had been waiting many years to receive. He could not contain his zest knowing that Lafty could become his adopted son, which was a dream they had prayed would become a reality one day, but he was not prepared for its impact. The excitement was far too much to handle on his own, so he made his way home to share the good news with his wife. Careful not to wake the boy he went into the room where he was sleeping to have another look at Sabuer. It was difficult for them to control their elation and for moment they were the happiest pair of people in the village. Their only fear was that someone would come to claim him. Thank goodness by then Sabuer was sleeping, even though it was mid-morning and the sun was glowing hot. Filled with emotion they left the house, sat on the steps leading up to the doorway and began to map out the little boy's future.

Having been a teacher Mrs Farkinson said, 'He is going be well educated and he will get the best of everything.' If Lafty's mother had heard those words how wonderful she would have felt knowing that her dreams were going to be fulfilled and that she could feel free of any guilt or blame. Mud also would have been very pleased at the result, because it seemed Lafty had found the right home.

As Lafty slept and Griff tried to accept his good fortune and come to terms with the rapid development of the day's events, his life story began to flash before his eyes. He could empathise with Lafty's plight, in particular the way he got there and the many questions that were surging through the little boy's mind. He had experienced a similar event that had taken him to that very island. It had happened many years past, he had been a young man in his twenties when he and his friends had gone on a fishing trip and got caught in a freak storm. Their little boat was smashed to pieces and they were left to battle against the mighty sea for hours until they reached the island where Griff now lived. The people there were very kind to them. They gave them a place to sleep, food to eat, clothes to wear, and the best care until the news of their safety reached their families on another island two hundred miles away and they came and took them home. While he had waited for his family to repatriate him from that unfortunate fishing trip, he met and fell in love with Elaina, a beautiful young islander, who was studying to become a Teacher. The time came for Griff to return home but he left carrying a heart that was heavily overflowing with love. Griff was twenty-three and Elaina was twenty, still a child by law. The distance between them became the dividing line that restricted any happiness they could have hoped for, and messages took months to travel across the sea. He didn't think he would ever get over the fire of love that burned inside him. It was a very agonising homecoming journey. Hope was all he had, so he prayed that one day he would make it back to the island and marry the girl he had left behind.

Griff and his friends arrived at their home town, another small village perched on the water's edge with fishing as their main source of food. Their arrival home after such a miraculous survival from an unforgiving sea was greeted with celebrations. The villagers and parents, rich and poor, saw them as heroes and welcomed them with opportunities to make all sorts of choices. Griff was invited to choose a wife from among the best and the glamorous, the educated or the illiterate, the rich or the poor. For a poor and un-educated person this was wonderful, he thought. But did he deserve the attention, he wondered, and would it make him happy? He had left his heart on that island; all he could do was to wait for the right moment. People began to wonder what was going on in his mind and began to talk in clusters of their disappointment. It seemed to them as if their daughters or sisters were not good enough for him. Who did he think he was, they wondered, ignoring their generosity? Griff appreciated their gesture but decided to wait and give time the chance to heal his broken heart.

For two agonising years he anxiously nurtured the wish to once more meet the girl that had stolen his heart. He was nervous of the sea, but the burden of love outweighed his fear. Griff decided to broaden his experience of the open sea as a sailor and not a fisher-man, working a ship that sailed between the islands, hoping it would help him to keep in touch with Elaina. But his ship rarely went to the island on which she lived, which was even more dis-turbing. Not having heard from her for a long time, his return home was met with exhilarating news that set his soul ablaze and rejuvenated every sagging limb in his body. Elaina had sent news that she had become a qualified teacher, an adult with power over her own future, and that her priority was the man she loved who lived two hundred miles away. He was dumbstruck and could not believe what was happening. Filled with excitement he went to find out to which port his ship was due to sail next. As fate would have it, he was told the ship would sail to the port of Elaina's home.

The ship set sail the following day, bound for the village port in which Elaina lived. It was a journey of two days, and Griff was a very happy man. Arriving at the headland, he had a clear view of the island being lapped by clear blue water, its layers of white and golden sands inviting him to note the spectacle of the mountains towering over the land as guardians to its inhabitants. The quilted patterns of the ripening leaves and the sweet-smelling fragrance that filled the air, combined with the joy of the shining sun and the invigorating sounds of the tropical birds completed his satisfaction of being there.

Gradually the ship edged closer and closer to the shallows of the village and dropped its anchors, and his heart leapt into action, busily carrying out his shipboard tasks, lowering the service boats for the transportation of goods and people to the pier head. Griff could not resist the temptation to jump ship for the girl of his dreams. He had been preparing for that moment since he left the island. He knew he could hardly walk into her life unexpectedly, a stranger with no means of supporting himself, and expect her parents to accept him with open arms. So Griff had taken all his savings, plus all that he earned working on the ship, and was ready to marry the girl he loved, whether or not her parents agreed.

On his first trip in the link boat to the pier head, Griff went to see Elaina's father and asked for his daughter's hand in marriage. It was a forgone conclusion. Her parents had suspected Griff would behave as he did, because love was the driving force and that for Griff to hold his bride was all that mattered. If only he could marry her there and then, he thought. But he had to be patient and allow her parents to organise what they saw was the best day for their daughter and them. Griff had to sit back and let his adopted family arrange at length what he wanted done in forty-eight hours. In the meantime the ship gently slipped its moorings and sailed to another island, less one sailor who had quietly hidden from those that sought him out. While the plotting and scheming went on at Elaina's parents' home, she was busy at the village school teaching a class of forty-plus children to read and write. There was no set age limit for learning, she taught them as they came whether they were five or fifty-five. Provided they had a passion to learn, they were welcome. Her motto was, 'No one is better than the other.'

That afternoon, while she was teaching, a member of the village came into the school and broke the exciting news of Griff's visit to her home. She had known he was coming to the island but had not known when he would arrive. It was the kind of news she had always wanted to hear, as it is every girl's dream to marry the she loves. Words could not adequately describe how she felt. Sick with excitement, her stomach churned in nervousness. She wanted to run to him, hold him, and tell him how much she loved him, but she was a teacher and respect and control were part of her remit. If she had never loved in her life that day certainly made up for those lost. As of that moment Elaina began to count the minutes to home time. Her body was an unwanted mass of goose pimples but her heart was safe in Griff's arms.

Their behaviour when they first met had created talk among villagers that one day they would get married and if the truth was to be known Elaina parents had helped to fuel those rumours. Griff had been loved by the villagers from the moment he had been rescued on their shores and when he left they had hoped that he would return to make their daughter his wife. She did not need anyone to tell her what Griff would do or was going to do at her house. She already knew he was going to talk to her parents about their friendship, but she had no idea that marriage would be on the table at that early stage. That afternoon's teaching session became the longest she had ever experienced; the clock seemed to have gone into reverse mode.

Soon the news began to filter through to the children's ears, saying 'Miss Elaina is going to get married.' Laughter became commonplace as a chain of whispered messages engulfed their minds and distracted their attention. Elaina's embarrassment was overwhelming to say the least. Her nerves were about to let her down and she could not hide her blushes; control was fast slipping her grip. 'Help me, God,' she whispered, wishing she could dismiss the class. But, while she sighed in desperation the head teacher, who had heard, came to her rescue.

Quietly, he said, 'I have heard your good news, so go on home and leave the classroom to me.'

She gathered her book, pencils and papers and quickly stored them in her cupboard, scrutinised by speculative eyes. Her pupils' smiling faces unnerved her. High off the ground in timeless motion, she stepped out, her head held proudly above the parting clouds. She did not look back as she floated through the tiny door. Her thoughts were adrift. 'Mrs Farkinson. Mrs Farkinson. What a wonderful name. How marvellous it sounds. If I should live to the end of time, I will love you, Griff.'

Her home was a mere half a mile from the school, so it would not take her long to face her demons –her mother and father, who she had not told how deeply in love she was. Elaina arrived home bursting to love Griff, and was gravely disappointed that he was not there. She found only the glowing faces of her waiting mother and father. 'Where is Griff?' she asked. Close to tears, she darted to her room and locked the door.

Griff had gone to meet the friends he had made, to share with them his future plans. He was a lucky man because Elaina's parents were not the richest people on the island, but then they were not among the poorest either. Her father was the son of a slave master and had been given an education, which put him into a more privileged position than many of his friends. He was also a member of the local governing body and commanded a great deal of respect. Her mother was a nurse at the village hospital and had delivered many of the village babies. Elaina was their only daughter. Her happiness was their priority and they were not going to have her marry anyone who could not care for her in the lifestyle to which she had grown accustomed. Many men from the island had made approaches to her parents for her hand in marriage and had been refused.

Griff did not have a respectable job, nor did he have land. He was not from a wealthy family, he was a fisherman turn sailor. But they must have seen something in him that suited the happiness of their daughter to be so ready to embrace him into their family. Yet Elaina had not at any time discussed marriage with her parents. In fact she was somewhat unsure of their reaction and avoided the subject whenever it arose during conversation. For the first time the table was clear for her to talk about marriage, which was the only way she felt she could be together with Griff.

While Griff waited with open arms for time to pass and for Elaina to return home from school, his wife-to-be was already at home, busily putting the final touches to their wedding day arrangements. Her mother and father had given their blessing for a happy and fruitful marriage and agreed that they should live with them. The momentum of that day was far too fast to take in what was happening. If anyone had told her that her parents would have been so readily agreeable she would have been very doubtful. That evening Griff returned to find all his marriage plans worked out, and within a few weeks the official ceremony was performed. Elaina became Mrs Elaina Farkinson and since that day no one addressed in any way other than Mrs Farkinson. They became a very happy couple and no one came looking for Griff, the man who had skipped his ship.

Griff took work where he could and over the years bought himself a beautiful boat, fulfilling his dreams. His wife, Mrs Farkinson, continued teaching at her local school. But tragedy has a way of appearing at unexpected moments. One day as she merrily made her way to the classroom, she fell and injured her back, resulting in constant, agonising pain that was frightening for Griff. He thought she had broken a bone. Several trips were made to the mission doctor who could do very little to arrest the excruciating pain that had taken over her life. She was forced to stay home and it seemed an end to her career. As a devoted husband Griff could not leave her on her own, so he sold his beautiful fishing boat and stayed home to care for his wife.

Their greatest disappointment was that they had no children. It was something they had looked forward to but it was never to be. So, when Griff brought Lafty into her home, with no one knowing who he was or where he came from, the clouds of dismay suddenly lifted from her wishful thoughts and instilled hope in its place. They had been married for thirty years and throughout that time they had never given up hope, even though her biological clock had run out of time where having babies was concerned. Was Lafty's presence a miracle gift? According to the boy's history, every indicator pointed to that conclusion. Lafty could only hope that over the years inquiries would be made of Ruben, his father, and his friends, Mud, Dusty and Scruffy, names that were the only clues for finding his roots. And if a choice had been given as to who might fit the idea role of parents for Lafty, without doubt the Farkinsons were the answer. They were a stable couple who yearned for the day they could have a child. Mrs Farkinson was a teacher with an ocean of experience in understanding children and their needs. Griff was a gentle person who wore love on his sleeve, and had the time to develop a well-structured life for Lafty. They had their own home and he would be well provided for; what better qualities could anyone have asked for in parents? Lafty would be extremely fortunate to have those people as his adopted parents; they would certainly have fitted Marybell's dreams and aspirations. She had been determined that her son should be spared from the brutality of slavery and knew the importance of an education which would enable him to take and make informed choices. Given the chance to stay with these people, Lafty could fulfil his mother's dreams. Mrs Farkinson would teach him to read and write and probably develop his speech. What better prospect could a mother have asked for her child at a time when everything seemed doomed?

Though Griff tried to stay away from the house to allow the women to settle the boy, he was as excited as any other given his situation. He wanted to believe that God was on their side and that what he had experienced was real and not an old wives' tale. More than anything he wanted to see Lafty, or to be more precise, Sabuer, which was his new name. Unable to stay still, he made his way back to the house after discussing every possibility of his miraculous encounter with his friends.

On his way he thought of a name for the little boy. How about Lucky? No, that was not strong enough for his son. What about James, or William the Conqueror, that was a good name, he thought. He would name him after his grandfather, Solomon the wise man. Yes that was right. He would settle for Solomon. He hoped Mrs Farkinson would like it as well. 'But surely,' he told himself, 'surely he must have a name. So why won't he tell us? That is very puzzling. He probably knocked his head in the storm and became forgetful. We'll have to take him to the doctor and have him checked out. Hopefully by then he will remember his name and put an end to all this speculation.' Griff reached his home and was greeted by his neighbour, Mrs Fagan.

'Be quiet,' she said, 'the little man is sleeping.' But the sound of his voice brought Mrs Farkinson to the door. She was radiant, content and happy. Surprisingly, she was walking upright, not arching, or holding on to anything for support, nor was she showing any sign of the back pain that had plagued over the years. What was happening, Griff wondered. Where had her back pain gone? That was his second puzzle in a matter of hours. He wondered if there was a message to be had.

'Come into the other room, Griff,' she said, 'I have something to tell you.' Exhausted from a confused morning, Griff followed her into the second bedroom. 'Close the door and sit down, I don't want to wake the little man, he's asleep in our room.'

Expecting the worst, he said, 'What have I done wrong? Shouldn't I have brought the lad home? I am sorry, but I did not have any-where else to take him. And I thought you would like the company.'

'Oh no,' she replied, 'that's okay. I love him, and thank you. You're too good to me, Griff Farkinson.'

'So what is wrong?'

'Nothing, my love. I have something very important to tell you. I have thought of a name for the little man.'

'What would that be?'

'I gave him the name Sabuer. I love that name and seeing as I did not know his real name, I had to give him a name. Do you think the name fits?'

Griff was stumped and could answer. He, too, already had a name prepared for Lafty, but his wife had beaten him to the punch.

'Say something, Griff. Your thoughts are equally as important. After all, he is our son.'

'Well, I was thinking of Solomon, after my grandfather. But if Sabuer is what you want, then Sabuer will be his name. But what if he begins to talk and tells us his real name?'

'Then, we'll just have to change it and make our name his second name.'

'That is one of the reasons why I love you so much, Griff. You're so understanding.'

Crowned in contentment, they emerged on the doorstep wearing an infectious smile as they introduced the new identity of their miracle baby to Mrs Fagan, who had patiently waited for their appearance.

'His name is Sabuer, Mrs Fagan.'

'That is a very unusual name, Mrs Farkinson.'

'Yes, Mrs Fagan, so it is. What you must remember is that he is a very unusual boy, Mrs Fagan.'

Griff sat in silence while both ladies locked in combat planning Sabuer's future. The events of that day were very confusing and no one could be complacent nor dismiss the strength of suspicious minds. Miracle or no miracle, nothing added up.

The midday sun stood high in the sky, its energy nourishing

growth and brightening up the landscape, while the refreshing breeze of the Caribbean waters ventilated their homes and cooled their bodies. Lafty lay asleep, oblivious to the plans of his adoptive parents. One by one the fishermen returned, having heard the news, and made their way to Griff's home. With gifts of clothes and homemade toys they gave their best wishes to their dear friend, convinced it was a miracle. And the more they talked of miracles the more plausible their experience became. Awash with happiness, Griff and his wife prayed the day would never end, just in case it was a dream. If only that miracle could see them though, what a wonderful end it could bring to their life. Mrs Farkinson knew it was all as real as real could be, and nothing could change what had happened.

Mrs Fagan wanted Mrs Farkinson to rest her back in case it flared up again, thinking that rushing around could make it worse. But Mrs Farkinson would not budge. 'For thirty years I have waited for something unexplainable to happen, and now it has, you must let me enjoy it in case I should die.'

'Don't talk like that, Mrs Farkinson. God loves you and he sends that little boy to remind you of that fact.'

'You are right, Mrs Fagan,' Griff said.

'Thank you, Griff,' said his wife. 'You always know how to make me feel good. Come here let me hug and kiss you for the wonderful present you brought home this morning. I can't explain those rumbling feelings that are inside. I know the boy is not my child, another mother gave birth to him, but I feel as though I am his mother, and he has been with me all along. Am I wrong?'

How strange life can be, Griff thought. While they sat and waited for news of any shipwreck, Sabuer cried out, making a strong yet frightening noise and sending all three pairs of feet rushing to the door. But when they got to him he was sleeping. He was probably dreaming of his experiences. The sound of his voice gave Mrs Farkinson hope. She was pleased because it gave her hope that the one day the boy would remember and would speak. 'He has a voice,' she said. 'That is wonderful. It might take him a long time to remember his name and where he came from, but in the meantime I'll teach him new things, and I have the time to do whatever it takes to make him a good, strong, intelligent person. Everything is going to be alright.'

Griff looked at his wife and thought, 'Is she going mad? Please God, he said to himself, I couldn't cope.'

Once again the little boy cried out loud and woke from his dreams, sitting up in the bed. 'This bed is very comfortable,' he thought. 'It's not like the straw-filled mattress aboard the ship and it's much better than my mother's. I could live here until my father comes to take me home.'

In went the three strange grown-ups, arguing about the right words to say to a frightened boy, a frightened boy no one knew. 'Hello, little man. Did something frighten you from your sleep?' said Mrs Farkinson. Are you thirsty? Maybe you are hungry? Can you remember your name?'

Questions followed by more questions was what he could do without. Lafty smiled and nothing was said. So again she asked she asked, 'Are you thirsty?'

The smiling lad nodded his head. And like a flash Mrs Fagan hurried back with a mug of water and handed it to Mrs Farkinson to feed the lad. His eyes were aglow with surprise. The mug was clean, with no chips in sight, he could not believe he was no still on board the ship drinking from his father's badly chipped mug. His brain was in turmoil. Nothing seemed real. One day he was among a bunch of rough-looking men, the next he had found himself on a comfortable bed with three nice people fussing over him. They did not look like cut-throats or slave masters. They seemed kind and caring just like his mother, he thought. Lafty held his side as though he was in pain and the observant Mrs Farkinson was quick off the mark.

'Is it your side that hurts?' she asked. She knew he was feeling pain. She went from the room, called out for Griff and he joined her on the front porch. 'Our little boy is in pain, Griff. 'Let's take him to the mission house and see the doctor.'

The frightened Griff called for his big strong fisherman friend to help carry Lafty to meet the doctor. In the meantime the two ladies dressed Lafty in the gifts of new clothing he had earlier that day and in a very short time they began the one mile journey to the mission house. Surprised though he was, Lafty understood all that was being said and done. Though he was a twelve-year-old, he was small in build and was not heavy, making him easier for the men to carry.

It was clear to the men that the boy could not be carried in their arms; wherever on his body he was touched it hurt. So they got a chair and tied two poles beneath the seating, using the protruding ends as shoulder carriers. He was then seated on the chair and elevated to shoulder height was carried the mile journey like a king on his throne. This was much more comfortable and within an hour they had reached their destination. Luckily the doctor was there and they did not have to wait for hours or days. The little boy was seen immediately. He was thoroughly checked, and the doctor not only checked his cuts and bruises he also checked his ears, nose and throat. Mrs Farkinson also told the doctor that the little boy had lost his speech.

An hour later, after a nervous wait the doctor explained to the Farkinsons that Lafty's ribs were badly bruised but not broken. He also had a deformed voice box but with careful training he would be able to speak, probably not as clear as might normally be expected, but clear enough to understand what he said. More importantly, the doctor told them his hearing was perfect. That was great news, not only for the Farkinsons but for Lafty. His hearing was perfect, his speech would get better with practice; there was nothing stopping him from fulfilling his mother's dreams.

Mrs Farkinson was delighted that she had been given a challenge that was dear to her heart. She knew that if she taught him to speak he would be extremely grateful and even though she could not be his biological mother she could play a very important role in his life for many years. The doctor had given her two parcels of powder that she had to give Lafty; one that night and the other the following night. All her aspirations seemed to bloom at the same time, and the miracle did not seem as far fetch as she had thought. Not only did she suddenly find herself with company, she also had a challenge in her classroom. She also had someone to distract her thoughts from the pain she sometimes endured. Griff, she thought, would have a playmate and more time for his fishing hobby without having to worry for her as he normally did. Their feeling that day was as warm, fulfilling and exhilarating as the day they got married. If only her parents could have shared their joy.

The two men got Lafty back on the chair and with a celebrating smile they made their way home, carrying that which no amount of money could buy. Lafty was a lot happier. He knew that he was in good hands and, whether or not his father came early or late, he had a good place to live. He was feeling good; sitting at shoulder height with a bird's eye view of the village as they paraded through the streets, giving him a clear and uninterrupted observation platform. This is going to be my home for a long time, he thought. But he could not help but think that his father should have found him by then.

They arrived home feeling strong and positive, having been reassured by the doctor's findings, comforted that the pain they bore for a child they could not conceive had rewarded their sufferings. They were also happy that the doctor had confirmed that their suspicion was wrong, that Lafty could hear and understand what was being said, and would probably speak soon. It put a lot more fun into their parenting role. Mrs Farkinson was a new person. She felt as though she had never been sick. She was strong and ready to tackle any problems. Griff was the quiet one. He just kept smiling, mesmerised by this colossal invasion that had reached into every corner of his unassuming lifestyle and left him wondering what was going on in his wife's head. Would she continue to love him as she had over the years? They had landed the jackpot, or to be precise, he had landed her the jackpot. In one clean sweep all their dreams had become a reality.

The impossible often happens and people accept it as being wonderful but unexplainable, and each passing day they become more and more thankful for their reward. It must have been that way for the Farkinsons, because it was too early to declare what had happened to them as a miracle or otherwise. However, the villagers were ready to regard the incident as nothing less than a miracle. It was in the villagers' interests to make a fuss, especially for those with their own self interest at heart. They wanted to see the village as a place of unimaginable phenomena, where people from miles around could visit and bring in wealth and prosperity. Whether or not Mrs Farkinson wanted to endorse their plans or accept their beliefs, it was inevitable, and sooner or later she and her family would become part of it all. People began to gather around them as they marched towards their home. It was a small crowd, but marked the beginning of what was to come. Everyone wanted to be identified with this unique couple. Beneath the surface, history was in the making, and Christianity was its underlining them. There was even talk that Christ would be the next to appear on their island.

While the village celebrated the promise of help for their new neighbour, Griff and his wife Mrs Farkinson carried a heavy burden of guilt. It was a haunting responsibility which was eating them away on the inside and one they would probably take with them to their grave. They were plagued by crippling thoughts that could never be properly prepared for, of the day when Lafty would speak and remember his name; remember his mother and tell the story of where he was from. What would be worse would be if he decided to return to his home and family. That, they thought, would be much worse than having lived without a child. The burden could put an end to either one of their lives. Every step of the journey was being paved with these sorrowful thoughts. Would Lafty love them enough to stay with them? Would he prefer his family over them? Losing him might cause more devastation than their life was worth. Such a happening would disrupt a tranquil community and take away the magical injection of hope and happiness.

The gathering reached their home and, without being told, surrounded the house in a massive show of strength, linking hands in friendship, and forming a chain of support and admiration. Lafty was gently lowered from his chariot and carefully taken into the house and put on the bed. Suffering less pain and feeling special to have been given so much attention, he smiled in happiness. Like bees to the honey pot everyone wanted to know how he was feeling. But how could they? He had not spoken of how he felt. No one except Mrs Farkinson knew the truth, that he could not speak as they would have liked to hear, and the little boy's smiles keep them happy in the knowledge that he was not unduly distressed. Although Mrs Farkinson had never been a mother, it was surprising how effortlessly her maternal instinct automatically sprang into action. She was very quick to clear the room of all strange faces and those whose services were not as important, leaving her and her friend Mrs Fagan to nurse her little boy. Knowing that Lafty could hear and understand what she said, she kissed his forehead and whispered in his ear, saying, 'Don't worry, I understand everything, and no one will ever hurt you as long as I live. You just lie down and rest. I will tell them that your name is Sabuer. That is until you can tell me what your mother calls you. Is that okay, Sabuer?'

The little boy held her hand and smiled as the emotion of love, joy and sadness cascaded through her thoughts and sparked a torrent of tears down her smiling cheeks. Mrs Farkinson was no longer a woman suffering a lengthy spell of excruciating pain from an injured back; she had become a vivacious person that was looking forward to an exciting tomorrow.

She made her way to the sitting room where many of the gathering crowd were sitting; each one frantically fanning their faces with anything that was within reach. Some used paper, some used cloth, and some flapped their hands while others used leaves from the flower garden. The sun was smiling brightly. Her watery face alarmed their thoughts. What could have made her cry? Something terrible had happened, they said, and total silence filled the room. She walked out on to the porch where her husband stood. He was there for her regardless of how she felt.

Locked in a world of thoughts and emotions he considered the day's events. Had he been chosen or was he mistaken? His confused mind could not separate the two. Hugged by a wife with similar feelings she held his hands and kissed his lips. 'I love you Griff,' she softly whispered. His heart raced as they hugged and he thanked God, and the others, for all their help and support. 'Where did you put Sabuer's medicine?'

'It's on the table,' he replied.

She loosened her grip and walked inside to search for the medicine that would make her boy well. No one knew why she was crying, and the silence was only broken by the flapping cloths, leaves, and fingers that kept their heated faces cool. On the table, just as he had said, she found the medicine neatly stored in its paper wrapping. One dose now and one dose tomorrow as the doctor said should make him better. 'Please God, make it work,' she whispered. She emptied the content into glass full of water, returned to the bedroom and said, 'Sabuer.' But the little boy did not move or acknowledge her. She was puzzled but quickly realised it was the name. Maybe she thought it was too early for him to accept a new name. 'Right little man,' she said, here is some medicine the doctor says should get you better. Be a good boy and drink it all for me.'

It was then he had realised she was using his new name and he had to remember it from there on. Little did she know that she had made a very good impression on him. She reminded him of his grand uncle's wife who was a very kind and loving person. Mrs Farkinson expressed a similar attitude, which he loved. He felt sure he would like it there if they could not find his father. She helped him to sit up and drink the dissolved powder that had a foul smell and taste. His face screwed up as he swallowed the last drop, but luckily Griff was at the door with a peeled orange for him to eat and take away this unusually bad taste from his mouth. Nothing more was said and for a while they sat with him until he slowly drifted into sleep.

Griff returned to his place on the porch and Mrs Farkinson sat with Mrs Fagan and others in the sitting room. 'We will have to speak quietly and let the lad sleep,' she said. She did not explain her reason for crying and no one dared ask. However, out on the porch, the men took a different view. They wanted to know why Mrs Farkinson was crying. 'Was the boy okay?' someone asked. They also wanted to be reminded of his name and wondered who it was that had given him that unusual name.

'It's all down to my wife,' said Griff, 'and I support her in everything she does.' The men congratulated him and his wife and promised to help in whatever way they could. Griff's eyes became watery with joy having heard his friends give such a powerful endorsement. All that he could hope for was that no one came to clam the boy; that they would be left to become the parents they had always wished to be. 'Regardless of how long he stays with us or who comes to claim him, we are going to enjoy every minute of being a father and mother figure in his life.'

'Good on you,' someone shouted as laughter filled the air. The jubilant nature of the gathering soon attracted the entrepreneurial zeal of a peanut vendor, who thought he could do some business there. 'Peanuts,' he cried repeatedly, but to no avail. So the whistling wind gave him a hand and blew that seductive and inviting smell of roasted nuts to titillate their taste buds and send their stomach rumbling. But his arrival brought dismay, no one seemed interested, nor was it the right atmosphere for selling. So he put down his load and sat with the men wanting to know what had happened to bring them there. Griff's friends told him the story; that the little boy lay sick in bed and could not remember his name. Overcome by the little boy's story, the peanut vendor gave away every last one of his freshly roasted peanuts, as a gesture of kindness, hoping that the little boy would recover and become part of their community. In deep gratitude, Griff and his friends accepted the vendor's compassionate outlook and enjoyed his fare. The Farkinson household had had its fair share of undiluted kindness.

For Elaina and Griff Farkinson the impossible had landed on their doorstep and changed their lives forever. The childless mother was at the heart of every conversation. Despite the fact that she had cared for more children at any given time than all her friends put together, she was at centre stage and had to listen and learn the secrets of parenting. Everyone knew of her desire to mother children of her own and knew that she had been denied that blessing. The child that came into her life was a gift that should be seen and accepted as God had intended.

Sabuer had gone past the age of twelve, way past the nursing stage. He had reached an age when he would begin to develop his own identity. Teaching a twelve-year-old was one thing; parenting a twelve-year-old was completely different and those of her friends with children of that age and over were ready to give advice. She was very encouraged by their interpretations of being a good mother, their advice enlightened her understanding of the behavioural development of her pupils. There was very little she needed to know about behaviour, it was behind-the-scenes interaction that was of interest.

That evening the sun slipped over the horizon, leaving the darkening sky to the twinkling stars that would soon appear there in their millions. The foreshore came alive as sailors lit their oil lanterns and hoisted them high on their masts, brightening up the landscape in celebration of the gift to one of their citizens. It had been a tiring day and it was now time for the Farkinson's many friends to make their way home. One by one they walked away hoping that tomorrow would be a happier day. Their miraculous gift was sound asleep oblivious to the confusion his presence had created. Whether or not this child was the answer they had been waiting for, they had decided to sleep and let tomorrow judge the outcome.

The Farkinsons had always been very close but that night more than ever they had a lot to be thankful for, as their belief in their miracle became stronger with every tick of the clock. There they were, in the cool of the night, listening to the distant roar of the mighty sea that had been so kind to a little boy. The warning barks of watchful dogs warded off intruders, human or animal, while the crowing cockerels tried to express their dominance over a sleepy village, reminding its residents of the passing hours. It would have been easy for Griff and his wife to count their blessings, close their eyes and sleep. But they lived in a village where nothing as dynamic had ever happened. And what they believed was a miracle kept them awake, in a reflective mood, savouring a moment they could easily have missed. They also knew that, awake, they would be on hand should they be needed to comfort the boy's troubled mind, if during the night he should wake in fright.

They thought they were the only ones that could not sleep, but across the village the lights burned brightly keeping a vigil for the little boy's recovery. All through the night cockerels crowed and left the villagers with wandering thoughts. Was there a message those birds were trying to convey?

CHAPTER 12

New Identity

Sabuer slept throughout that night and woke as the rising sun shone through the open window. 'Good morning, Sabuer,' said Mrs Farkinson as she walked into the room, her beautiful smile lightening her happy face. 'Did you sleep well? You must have been very tired.'

His sparkling eyes were ablaze as though it was his mother that had entered the room. Mumbling sounds parted his lips as he answered the lady, his new mother, so he thought. Mrs Farkinson did not need an interpreter. She knew instantly what the little boy was saying. To her delight it was, 'Good morning Mother.' She had the answer to her troubled mind.

'Come in here, Griff, and say hello to Sabuer; he's awake.'

Griff hurried into the room excitedly and said, 'Good morning, little man.'

'No, no, his name is Sabuer.

Griff corrected himself, 'Good morning, Sabuer.'

The little boy's lips opened wide, revealing a set of sparkling white teeth that lit up his face and filled the room with laughter. 'This is a happy boy if ever I have seen one, Mrs Farkinson. And how is your side, Sabuer, does it hurt?'

Sabuer touched his bandaged ribs and shook his head, saying, 'No, sir, it doesn't hurt.'

'You have heard him, Griff. You are now a father, so start acting like one. Your son needs a hot drink and so do I.'

With the room ablaze with smiles and happiness, Griff was in a different world. A new life had begun. It was a new beginning, not only for his family but for the islanders, because nothing could ever be the same. He went to kitchen and made the hot drink, but before he had finished Mrs Fagan arrived. She, too, had been worried for the little boy's safe recovery and had not slept.

'Come inside, Mrs Fagan. The little man is smiling as usual and there is no sign of any pain.'

'Well done little man, thank God you're better,' she replied.

'Until he says differently, Mrs Fagan, his name is Sabuer. I must also tell you that Sabuer is very shy, and does not speak much, so don't expect many answers. You'll understand, won't you, Mrs Fagan?'

'Yes, Mrs Farkinson, that is clear. I do understand. Sabuer and I are going to get on just fine.'

'His health has certainly improved, Mrs Fagan, much more than I was expecting. At this rate, it won't be long to a full recovery, wouldn't you agree, Mrs Fagan?'

'Yes, Mrs Farkinson. All I can say is that you have finally got your son. Thanks to Jesus.'

'I thank Him as well, Mrs Fagan.'

Twelve hours had passed and the likelihood of the boy becoming their son was firmly established in their household. The emergency of his health had been successfully been dealt with; now his legal status was the agenda.

'Griff,' said Mrs Farkinson, 'you have to go to the police station and ask the Sergeant to call on me. Let's get things straight. I am concerned that Sabuer's parents could have been part of the ship-wreck. They could either have been rescued or else someone might know something. Whichever is the case, we are obliged to inform the law and register his name and present address.

'That's a very good idea. I'll get onto it soon.'

'Yes, Mr Griff,' said Mrs Fagan. 'Why don't you get one of your friends to go with you; like the one that helped you yesterday.'

'You're right, Mrs Fagan. Good thinking.'

While Griff continued his conversation with Mrs Fagan outside the house, Mrs Farkinson and Sabuer were locked in a bonding ritual, getting to know each other. She was very anxious that Sabuer knew as quickly as possible how much she knew about him. Also, that he knew what the doctor had told her, that although he had not been able to speak properly in the past, it did not mean he would not speak well in the future. Those words brought tears of joy to his eyes and gave him a steely confidence.

'I am a very good teacher,' she said. 'I can understand what you say. I don't want you to be afraid to talk to me, and you can use any method you wish.'

Mrs Farkinson began to use her illness to reassure Sabuer that he too could do whatever he set his mind to, because she was capable and willing to help make it happen. 'I have been a good teacher for many years, until one day I fell and injured my back. I have tried to teach since, but the pain had been unbearable. I couldn't walk or stand, and everyday it seemed to get worse than the day before, so I had to stay home. But I'll tell you something that I find uncannily amazing. Since you came into the house, which is about twenty-four hours ago, I haven't felt a pinch of pain and I have been standing, walking, almost running. I can't remember the last time I have been without pain for more than one hour, let alone twenty-four. Isn't that wonderful? You have brought more than the happiness of a passing dream, your presence has given a new purpose to my life, and I love you very much.'

Sabuer listened, but with a puzzled look on his face, as if to say, 'Why are you telling me this?'

'I know I must sound like a silly woman, but I want you to be happy and not to feel strange. More importantly, I am going to teach you to read and write so that you can write the words you have difficulty saying. How about that, Sabuer?'

By this time he had got used to his new name and had accepted it as though it had always been used. Sabuer held her hand, lifted himself onto the bed and hugged her. Wrapping his hands around her neck he buried his face into her shoulder. The joy of the little boy's breath on her neck sent her into a fit of laughter and this startled Griff, who quickly came to see what was wrong. That little boy's emotions were far-reaching. It was a moment of sheer happiness as he expressed the joy of two people. He was extremely pleased with her promises, knowing that they were also his mother's wishes. If only she could understand his thoughts to know how thrilled he was that she had been behaving exactly as his mother.

Sabuer knew that from there on that he would become a very satisfied person, and that everything his mother had promised was about to be fulfilled, and that the Farkinsons would always have a son. There was no need to worry for his future, whether or not his father turned up. He had not found the aunt he had been sent to, but he had found someone who thought and acted like his mother.

The satisfaction of that moment seemed like a lifetime of exuberance. Nothing could change how she felt about the son she had been mysteriously given. She was also experiencing inner changes that could not be explained at a stroke. There was no pain, or discomfort. The injured back that had put a stop to her teaching career and prevented her from having a normal existence had become a distant memory. Whether or not it could be proven that this mysterious phenomenon had brought with it some healing power; it was without doubt that the healing process had taken place.

Her relaxed approach was certainly affecting Sabuer. He was trying to express his thoughts, perhaps even his name. It was a joy to her soul, and she made every effort to understand the movement of his hands and the way he chose to describe what he wanted to say. She clearly understood he was talking about a ship, a big storm with lots of things being broken and someone tying him to something, which, as she knew, was the broken mast. However, she could not work out what he was saying of his friend. The sound of 'mud' did not make any sense to her. There was no mud aboard the ship, she thought. Unable to communicate his explanation of 'mud', perhaps Sabuer became tired. He did not realise that his new mother could not understand him as quickly as his biological mother had. Like most kids of his age he got bored and got up from the bed, proving that his strength had returned. At first he hopped, then after a few steps he began to walk around the room, looking at the beautiful furniture that had taken every inch of space. The thought of occupying a room such as that set his brain buzzing. It was a tempting thought. He could not be that lucky, could he?

But there was no one else living in that house so far as he could see, and if he stayed with them, whether or not his father came, the room could become his. What would he call her, he thought, not that he could speak plainly, but 'Mama' was not a hard word to say. 'Maybe I'll call her Mama,' he thought to himself, 'She might like it.'

It appeared that Mrs Farkinson had been reading his mind, because by the time he had walked back to the bedside where she sat, she said, 'For now you can call me 'Mum' and Griff 'Papa', which I think is easy for you to say. Is that okay with you?' she asked. Sabuer nodded his head, smiling, leaving her a little nervous that her motherly enthusiasm was too much too soon. As though the clock had missed a tick, the little boy's mouth let loose a magical cacophony of sounds, which she took as laughter. But she was not sure why he was laughing. Was he rejecting her?

In truth it was his way of saying that he loved her and had already decided that she looked and behaved like his mother and if they would have him he would love to stay with her and Griff. The little boy tried to wrap his hands around her in a sign of solidarity and affection.

As a teacher Mrs Farkinson knew how to control a child's emotions. Her attention was firmly fixed on the many gifts Sabuer had been given and she began to search through the various parcels to see what was inside. He needed to get dressed and make himself pre-sentable even if only for his neighbour, Mrs Fagan. In among the parcels she found a smart pair of trousers and a blue shirt which was twice his size but good enough to wear around the house.

In the beautiful basin that he admired with interest Mrs Farkinson washed his hands and face, took a quick look at his cuts and bruises and was satisfied at their healing progress. Deep inside her emotions stirred. Was this real or was she dreaming, she wondered. She took him to the sitting room and joined Mrs Fagan, who by then had cooked a feast-like breakfast to celebrate the recovery of a special little boy. Sabuer was about to partake of his first full meal in his new home, so it had to be special.

As they sat around the table the thankful Mrs Farkinson said grace; a long and wonderful prayer. Their staple diet was fish and root vegetables, similar to that in his homeland, making the food enjoyable to eat. He was hungry, though not exactly starving he could eat more than his normal share. So he did, and this brought smiles to all three faces around him. While they ate as one big family it was hard to believe that twenty hours earlier Sabuer's life had hung in the balance and that news of his arrival had come like a tornado to the islanders. Before they could leave the breakfast table, curiosity brought a steady flow of people wanting to see this miracle boy. They gathered in numbers outside the house beneath the shade-less sun. It was hot and exhausting, but they waited patiently.

Mrs Farkinson explained, 'The little boy is unwell. Come back another day when he is better.' No one listened, and they all stood their ground. A few hours later Mrs Farkinson conceded and showed off her miracle son to the delight of everyone. During her teaching years she had had many exhilarating moments with satisfied parents, but at no time had she ever been as fulfilled as she was then. She felt humble to have been given such an accolade purely because of the presence of this unknown little boy. That day, and those feelings, became a continuous source of reassurance and encouragement for her to be thankful to the boy's mother for giving birth to him, to God for sparing his life, and to the sea for bringing Sabuer to her.

During the passing days the watchful eyes of vigilant villagers wished good health to their welcome visitor as his cuts and bruises healed and his inquisitive mind set to work exploring his surroundings. Haunted by a fear of the sea, he was convinced that his father was somewhere in its depth and that he was to be blame. The little boy thought he had brought bad luck to his father's ship. It would take a long time and plenty of persuading before he could become confident enough to swim in the sea.

The two ladies began to plan the boy's first public appearance, which they thought would be church. There were three days to go until Sunday and they would have to visit the shop and buy clothes that fit him properly. Even though he had been given gifts of clothing, it would not be right for him to wear other people's cast-offs to church. 'We must make him the envy of our village,' said Mrs Farkinson. 'He must be smartly dressed in case the police sergeant or the magistrate attends Sunday service. We don't want to give them any reasons to remark on his appearance.

'Yes, Mrs Farkinson, you are absolutely right.'

'Well then, Mrs Fagan, let's get to work and get the boy looking smart.'

The two ladies went to the city, scouring the stores to buy material for Sabuer's new look. They avoided buying any ready-made clothing in case it did not fit to their taste. The village tailor would do him proud, they thought. By the time they got home they had bought enough material to dress a classroom of children, let alone one small boy.

CHAPTER 13

Registration

The police sergeant's arrival came two weeks after Griff had reported Sabuer's rescue. His visit was at Mrs Farkinson's request, but to also see the lad and hear his story. By profession they had both been entrusted with the responsibility of their community, and enjoyed positions of great respect, which made them duty-bound to safe-guard individual needs. She explained to the police sergeant how the lad had come into their care, his injured condition and the urgency for medical attention. She also told him how willing she was to adopt the boy as their child, and called upon his caring nature to help in procuring her wishes.

But the sergeant's presence created terrifying moments of anxiety. Griff was afraid that the police sergeant might find reasons to remove the boy, before the magistrate decided on where he rightly belonged. Though it had been a month since they had met, the boy had become as precious to him as his wife. He was getting used to having a son, if only in name. If he should lose the lad, he thought, the shock might kill him.

Up until then the police sergeant had not heard of any ship-wrecks, which left him baffled. 'A few ships have called at the island ports,' he said, 'but no one has heard of this supposed wreckage. Furthermore, news of the boy has been sent to the masters of every plantation in the neighbouring islands. Whether or not this little boy was a runaway, no one can be sure.'

Thinking aloud, the sergeant suggested that maybe the boy was being taken away from his parents to another island and had jumped overboard when the ship got close to the island. The sergeant looked at the little boy and thought that an act of this kind could only have been committed by an adult and not a twelve-year-old who could not speak. He agreed there was no solution at present. 'But,' he said, 'you have to present the lad before the magistrate and have his name officially registered. Then it will be his judgement whether or not you keep him. Not as your child, but as guardians, until such time when everyone is satisfied that all enquiries have been exhausted. Then, and only then, could you become his adopted parents. However, this inquiry could take many years, by which time the lad could accept you as his parents and set aside the need for his biological parents until he could make enquiries of his own.'

The sergeant made a date for the Farkinsons to appear before the magistrate and straightened out any misunderstandings and fears. Pleased that he had brought hope into their lives, he went away. But his departure left Mrs Farkinson with mixed feelings. On the one hand she was happy that Sabuer would be registered, and that no one had yet made a claim on him. He was also happily finding his place in the community. But she was haunted by the fear that someone would recognise her boy. Like Griff, it was doubtful whether she could bear the disappointment of losing him.

While she pondered on her thoughts and watched her Sabuer heal after his ordeal, accepting his new home, two months swiftly passed, and it was time to attend the magistrate's court. They arrived at the courthouse, adjacent to the school in which she taught, a place she had visited on many occasions speaking on behalf of someone who could not articulate in a manner that would sustain their rights. She was not suffering from any strange or nervous feelings. Elegantly she presented her case and appealed to the magistrate to understanding. Having heard her plea, the magistrate was very sympathetic and pleased that she had had her dreams fulfilled in such an unusual way. He officially registered Sabuer in the care of Elaina and Griff Farkinson, with them as his as legal guardians.

Signing that register was exactly what they had wanted. Realising they were one step closer in becoming lawful parents, they thanked the magistrate, who, as it happens, was her uncle. They walked from the courthouse that day, their heads held high, proudly escorting their boy, Sabuer. The waiting group of celebrating friends greeted their arrival, while the cloudless sky witnessed the flood of joyful tears and satisfaction.

Though it was only a few hundred yards to their home, where they longed to be, outside the house there was a carnival scene as family friends and neighbours cheered them on, congratulating her miracle gift. It was time for Mrs Farkinson to appreciate what she had. Sabuer's presence had removed any doubt that a child might not have been the most precious gift to make their lives fulfilled. With her boy at her side she did not have to do anything other than to sit back. She became a guest in her home, was invited to sit on the porch and allowed her friends and neighbours to express their joy and happiness.

Without her knowledge, they had brought everything to create a feast, and turned her homecoming into something like a wedding banquet. They wanted to show how special she was to them having educated their children and so having helped them fulfil their own dreams. Her dedication to the education of the children of those families had been appreciated far more than she had imagined. The event gave her the perfect opportunity to finally and publicly display her feelings. She thought that the respectful acknowledgement and the many thank-yous she had received over the years was all that she had deserved. But that day she was astounded at the extent to which those people were prepared to show their gratitude. She was not on her own, either. The crowding mass had sent Griff and Sabuer into a compound state of elated shock and the little boy had no idea that it was all in his honour.

Although the island's people practised a constituted Christian ideology and worshipped at several well-established world mission churches that preached the gospel as it was written in the Holy Bible, there were those that practised other forms of worship. Some believed that there was more than one God and would worship as they were commanded. Many believed that their God was the strongest in granting its worshippers their wishes. The mysterious appearance of this little boy had created an enormous interest, causing everyone to try to unravel the reasons for his presence.

There was a strong feeling among parts of the community that, while their Gods were busily handing out powers to the faithful, a disagreement had occurred which had resulted in the boy's appearance, and that he held the key to further and higher powers. The people who thought this way were very keen to get close to the boy and test his magical powers. His mysterious survival caused them to believe that he could become their most powerful mystical leader, and so they used the general celebratory goodwill of all these Christian people as a cover for their own deceptive ideals. They regarded the Farkinsons' wishful dreams as unimportant to their vision.

Neither Griff nor his wife had any suspicion of their contagious attitudes and went about protecting their boy in the way they knew how. However, amid the excitement of eating, drinking, singing, dancing and plotting, Mrs Fagan suggested that Sabuer should be baptised, to evoke God's blessing on the boy. 'That is a very good idea,' said Mrs Farkinson. 'We had thought of it, but had not thought it urgent. Maybe we will after tonight.'

Whether or not Mrs Fagan knew that devil worshippers were trying to get to their son is not clear, but the forcefulness of her advice made the Farkinsons act quicker than they otherwise would have, and they planned the blessing of their boy at the following Sunday's church service. They were aware of those in the community that professed to be witches, with mystical powers that could allegedly heal the sick and cast away spells or evil spirits. It was not unusual to hear of their evil doings. But they did not know that it was the greatest wish of such people to regard their boy as a miracle sent by their God to lead them, and that that very night could mark the beginning of a new and profound change of attitude among the villagers, followed closely by the island as a whole.

Having been oppressed, beaten and demoralised in believing what they had been told by elders, many on the island were too frightened to question any unusual happenings. Perhaps the boy's mysterious arrival did have far-reaching consequences. Having been brainwashed by the mystical mumbo jumbo that had been pumped into their heads, many people on the island were terrified that to stand up to such ideas could bring misery upon their families.

This phenomenon gave the village's bush doctor a strident voice among the gathered crowd. It gave him scope to develop his magical powers and to create confusion in the minds of nervous people. Such thinking could creep across the island like a slow-burning fire. The boy's powers could bring about changes and strengthen their leadership. Those misguided people longed for the magical powers they thought the little boy possessed.

The Farkinsons and the Fagans were dedicated Christians who dismissed any forms of cult or devil worshipping from their door. They could only trust in their God, their church and their faith that He would protect their boy from the evil deeds of black magic.

Though Mrs Farkinson had enjoyed the generosity of that night, she was particularly pleased to see the dawning of a new day, and to share in the company of a loving husband and foster son. He was peacefully asleep after an exciting evening like nothing he had ever experienced. It was something for him to remember when we are no longer here, Mrs Farkinson thought.

Griff, too, was awake and happy with the family he had always wanted. 'What have we done to deserve that wonderful reception given to us by our friends?' asked Griff.

'Griffith,' replied his wife, 'You and I are blessed because we have done many good things to and for our friends, so it's their way of saying thanks. Griff, I have made Sabuer a promise which I intend to keep. Whether or not I am in pain, I will not let this lad out of my sight until he can speak, read and write, and that promise starts today.'

'What can I do to help?'

'Well, you will be able to spend more time with your friends or go fishing. It doesn't mean that I love you less; in fact I'll love you more. There'll be something exciting to share every time you walk through the door and he speaks to you.'

'I can't wait for that day, Mrs Farkinson.'

'Neither can I, Griff. Neither can I.'

It was time to put into action the promises she had made and remove from her thoughts the negative reactions of the witch-doctor's performance.

The morning sun greeted their positive thinking and Mrs Farkinson was once again in full control. She made the breakfast and Sabuer filled the empty chair at the table and made the family complete. They gave thanks for their blessings and ate their breakfast. Griff went out fishing, leaving the teacher to teach.

'Well, Sabuer, I am going to make sure you can speak, read and write.' Happy though she was at her friends' and neighbours' generosity, and the stupendous celebration that greeted her family that day, she was reminded of the promises she had made. It was time to put into motion the plans she had for her son. Without hesitation Mrs Farkinson began the preparations for her son's entry to the school.

The following six months bore testimony to her dedication. She was determined that her boy could read, write and speak before he was thrust into the full glare, for all to criticise or taunt his disability. It took her nine months of careful nurturing by which time Sabuer could read, write and speak, not as clearly as others, but plain enough for them to understand. This gave her peace of mind and encouraged his confidence in his own ability to communicate, making it easy for other children to treat him with equal attention. Her determination had paid off and her boy would not become a deliberate target for abusive taunts.

They were delighted that he was keen to pursue an educational future; early though it might have been, they could see that he had talent and could become whatever he set his sights on doing. Mrs Farkinson hoped that her boy would follow in her footsteps and become a teacher, carrying on the work she had begun all those years ago.

Taking Sabuer to school aged twelve-going-on-thirteen would be the fulfilment of her life's work. The school was crying out for her teaching skills, but her boy's interests came first, so Mrs Farkinson decided to allow her boy to settle down before she herself returned to her school. While she waited, the days became long and weary and she sometimes felt the odd sharp pain but only in passing. Sabuer settled into his new routine, learning at school and having his brain topped up with extra knowledge at home. Griff became a new man with plenty of time to fish. He walked with his boy and taught him nature's complexity, its produce and its ingenious method of recycling, completing the cycle of earth inhabitants.

However, the years were passing faster than Farkinsons had expected. Sabuer's days in that school were coming to their end and his educational standard was not up to her satisfaction. She was getting close to her sixtieth birthday and her fifteen-year-old boy needed a lot more education if he was to be equipped to make informed choices. At fifty-seven she went back to the school and helped her son to earn good exam results, and by the time her boy had reached eighteen he had passed every examination he had taken. He had also developed perfect speech.

Sabuer was growing into a fine young man with a great future ahead of him. No one had come to make a claim on him and the

Farkinsons were free to adopt him and give him the family name. Buried deep inside were memories of his mother and sister and father. If only he could be told whether they had lived or died. But he was nevertheless content that he was living his mother's dream. His zest for learning became a driving force. The Farkinsons did not have to tell him or remind him to study; more knowledge was what he wanted. Perhaps he was being driven by the wishes of his biological mother. He was not sure what profession he wanted, but whatever his choice of career he would have to first leave home to study at a college or university for three to five years, probably in another country.

As Sabuer prepared himself to leave the home, friends, and family he loved and begin to study for a career, his mother's aging body began to reject the increasing demands of her profession. It was time for her to sit back and enjoy Griff's company and occasionally gaze at her achievements with satisfaction. She had fought against illness and successfully fulfilled the promise she made to her son, which had placed him on the path toward his goal. Mrs Farkinson could be proud of her work. In seven years she had nurtured a boy that was friendly and kind. He had made many friends but did not seem to have a best friend, or someone that was closer to him than the rest. At eighteen he should have been exploring the unknown and experimenting with his identity but such things were of no interest. Instead, day after day his eyes would be buried in a book, and he was driven by the words he read.

He was also curious to know the true story of his survival, a subject that neither his Mum nor Papa spoke of in his presence. But his intelligence was increasing and it empowered him to make enquiries. Sabuer wrote letters to many Caribbean islands and other countries that owned shipping to seek out information on shipwrecks during the year he was rescued. Over the years he had been slowly gathered enough facts to make his own judgement on the exact nature of that disaster, but there was no guarantee that his assessment was correct. It was as if the motive for furthering his education was to discover the truth of his existence.

In order to achieve his goal he knew he would have to travel by ship to another country, America, and up until then he had not come to terms with the sea. He was terrified of a repeat occurrence, though could not breathe a word of his fears. What would they think, he thought? An intelligent young man living at the water's edge, listening to the roaring seas day and night, who was afraid of it? People would make a big joke of him, and it would be embarrassing. Even though on many occasions Griff had taken him fishing and they would travel up to a mile out to sea, Sabuer's phobia remained strong. It took a gentle nudge from those concerned and mountains of loving care to strengthen his confidence enough to make that journey. He was extremely nervous but could not reveal his true feelings, not without clouding the happiness that shone in the faces of those he loved.

His preparations brought on a twist of sadness, but Mrs Farkinson was not going to allow anything to sidetrack the importance of her boy's biggest decision. She sat in her favourite chair, with Griff beside her, and reminisced. 'Do you realise that it's going on seven years now that Sabuer has been with us? I have thought of him always here beside us, haven't you? Look at him, Griff, our son has grown so fast, and is so loveable. Soon he will be gone, leaving an empty chair.'

She could take comfort from the memories of those times she had spent apart from Griff while she had trained to become a teacher and he had returned to his parent's home. 'We must be getting old, Griff; soon we won't be able to move. But if we did it once, surely we could do it again? Griff, we owe it to our son to wait for him.'

Griff smiled, 'Yes dear, I'll do my best.'

As though she was telepathic, Mrs Fagan shouted across her garden edge. 'Your boy is going to leave us soon, Mrs Farkinson. Are you going to wait for his return?'

'Well, my dear Mrs Fagan, if it's the Lord's will, I will be here.'

'That's the spirit, Mrs Farkinson. We'll have a big party.'

Mrs Fagan's husband was a very talented sculpture who could carve beautiful pictures on wood. So he thought of giving the boy a going away present and set about carving a special necklace gift for Sabuer. Each link was a picture of bird, insect or animal, and he painted those subjects to match their natural colours. It was a masterpiece. The Fagans had done him proud. The necklace stood out in its elegance. Sabuer thought it was the loveliest thing he had ever seen and was overwhelmed. However, his Mum and Papa thought it made him look like a witchdoctor. Could they have been as superstitious? Their actions suggested they were. But was this specially-carved necklace as innocent as it seemed? Whether or not Mrs Farkinson was aware of anything untoward, she was not saying, which left a question mark between her and Mrs Fagan.

Mrs Farkinson had secured a place for Sabuer in one of New York's universities, where Sabuer could develop and become the educated person he yearned to be. The ship was already anchored in the bay and was waiting for the following day to sail. If all went to plan, Sabuer would be aboard for a journey of almost two weeks across the mighty Atlantic Ocean. No one slept that night. The Farkinsons and Fagans were worried for their boy's safety. Even though they had mentally prepared for that day, when the time came it brought all the shock, horror and distress of losing some-one special. Throughout the night the cockerel bird crowed and crowed as though someone had told it that Sabuer was leaving that day. With so much music they could not be late. Dawn broke amid the cacophony of singing birds and waking inhabitants. The two ladies had prepared his bags and given him their instructions so there was little else to do other than to wash, dress, and eat. Having made that journey some years before, Mrs Farkinson had some idea what awaited him, and her experience helped him to prepare his mind. Breakfast over, the Farkinsons, the Fagans and many others set off to shouts from well-wishers for a safe voyage.

Out in the bay the giant ship awaited its special cargo, the boy who had mysteriously survived the perils of an unforgiving sea. The harbour was too small for the ship to enter, so he boarded a small boat and waved goodbye to those he loved, hoping that lightning would not strike twice in the same place, and that he could return to Mum and Papa. Slowly, the small boat drifted towards the giant ship, riding the waves like a playful fish, though it was not so for Sabuer. Both his stomach and his head were at odds with feelings of weightlessness. Closer and closer the boat edged on its way, protected by a fleet of fishing boats, sounding horns, hailing the lad and bringing a great air of excitement to their homeland. Merrily the boat danced with the waves, carrying its passenger, his luggage and his ambition towards a new life.

He climbed onto the ship and was at last out of sight to his family and friends. As he stepped upon the deck, greeted by the glorious sun, the rolling ship reminded him of the past. He was not the only young man on board, there were others he knew. The education authority had organised the journey and had become responsible for their guidance. They queued to have their papers checked and Sabuer discovered that he was out of sight to the shoreline and the boats. This is it, he thought. It was no different from the day his father had taken him aboard his ship. He began to wonder whether the experience would be the same, but to his surprise things were entirely different. The ship was bigger, with more space, and had roomier cabins with comfortable beds and, best of all, a nicer smelling kitchen. He took his place alongside the others.

On shore, the Farkinsons and their friends watched and waited for the giant ship to lift its anchors. Time stood still as no one moved. The morning sun climbed into the midday sky lighting the corners of their beautiful land, but it is doubtful that Sabuer's family and friends saw it that way. They were too busy harping on about the past. Suddenly the ship's giant chains began slipping their way to the deck, raising the anchor and releasing the vessel. Slowly it moved towards the setting sun.

Reluctantly, the Farkinsons and their friends returned to their homes. Elaina and Griff were faced with an empty home that seemed lifeless; only a shell. Had they done the right thing? All their lives they had waited patiently; waiting to embrace a child that would see them through their passing days. But he had now gone from their grasp in less than seven years. Were they been selfish to want to keep him at their side?

'He'll soon be back,' Mrs Farkinson quietly whispered. 'Three more years and he'll become an adult. It will be a time we'll be proud to share, won't we, Griff?'

Griff wasn't answering. His thoughts were far away. They were floating out in the deep with his boy, and those sorrowful feelings lasted for what seemed a very long time.

The ship made good progress, crossing a trouble-free ocean and arriving on time two weeks later. Sabuer had reached New York, his new home where his sponsoring school had organised a waiting party to escort he and his fellow islanders to the seat of knowledge where he was prepared to make good use of his time. Journeying through the city was fascinating. He was mesmerised by the beauty of its high-rise buildings and shop window displays. He could not comprehend the richness of the city and thought this could be the place for him to live. In no time he could become wealthy, but would he be happy free from slavery, as he was in his country? He was already alarmed at the behaviour between black and white people, and for the first time he realised the awfulness and the indignity of slavery. First there was the separation between the races. He was put into a group of all black people, which was not of any great significance to him until he saw all the white people in another group by themselves.

They arrived at the university and once again he was shocked at its vastness. It was almost as big as his entire country. How long would it take him to find his way around the place, he wondered. By time he had, it would be time to return home. Having been given his placement, and a quick tour of the main buildings, he sat and looked at the historical place that was going to become his home for three to five years. Before he unpacked, he had to write a letter to his Mum and Papa and put an end to their wondering minds.

Dear Mum and Papa,

I have arrived at a place that is huge. It is almost bigger than our country. Everything here is on a large scale; buildings, roads, farms boats and people. The school is massive, with an enormous array of learning materials which I intend to take advantage of and make you proud when I return home. I miss you very much, but I'll be back in two to three years. That's not long, is it?

He could not bring himself to tell them of the segregation he was having to face, it would make them miss him even more. Sabuer held his nerve and kept his feelings private. Not knowing his way around, he went in search of the post office which, he was told, was situated in the main building. In his search he found his guardian, who gave him stamp and an envelope and his first letter was posted there and then. It was time for him settle down, accept their absence and wait for answer. He had three years to prepare for the career he wanted and live up to the standard he had set himself which he believed would make his parents proud.

CHAPTER 14

Joy and Sadness

Not long after being Lafty, the boy who could not speak, read or write, a disposable commodity, destined to a life of slavery as a disabled child, he had begun the routine his mother had prayed for. His mother's decision and the perilous sea had brought him to the house of knowledge and soon he would be taking and making decisions based on informed choices. His future was his. If he did well, he would be recognised for his achievements. It was a platform the Farkinsons had created and he was determined to make every effort to take advantage of their initiative.

For three long years he studied; harder and harder each year, passing every test and examination he faced. He wrote to his parents at every given opportunity and kept them up-to-date, and while they celebrated, he joyfully became better educated. He did not make time for anything else and soon his devotion had paid dividends. Three years was coming to an end, the knowledge he sought had been achieved and Sabuer had become a qualified teacher, just like his Mum. But he wanted it kept as a surprise. He would have liked to continue his studies and take advantage of the investment his country had placed in his education.

His greatest disappointment was the postal service. It sometimes took two months or more for an answer to reach him. And it was not because his mother was slow to answer. The weather conditions determined the speed at which ships could safely across the Atlantic Ocean; and how many ports they called at before reaching his country. His mother's letters were welcome when they arrived. Apart from the first letter that took close on three months to receive, the others flowed at a steady interval, keeping hope alive and letting him know that everyone was happy. It was an awesome time for Sabuer, he had achieved his first goal and was about to aim higher, when he received a very short letter, which contained disturbing news. The letter read simply, 'Your mother is very ill and is calling for you. Love, Papa!'

The news knocked the stuffing out of him. If only he had had wings he would have flown to her side there and then. Instead, he presented the letter to his college principal, and immediately organised a passage on the next available ship bound for Caribbean, hoping his Mum would still be alive when he got there. His fear of the open sea became a mere memory. After ten years the phobia that had haunted him simply disappeared. Could it have been another unexplained mystery or was it being masked by shock? Whatever it was, thank goodness the return journey took less than two weeks and he arrived to see his dying Mum, waiting as she had promised. It was the saddest day of his life. The hurt he felt when he saw the mother he loved lying helpless in bed was indescribable. Her bubbling personally had brought happiness and laughter to everyone she had met, and it seemed she was to have no chance of enjoying the reward of her hard work in nurturing him to become what he was. He was desperate for answers, but none were to be found, so he blamed himself for leaving her, which was far from the truth.

Although she did not suffer any of the excruciating pain she had felt before Sabuer had come into her life, she was never completely free of pain. The injury had done more damage than the doctors could tell. Her body struggled for its life, and like a newborn baby she wanted to kick and scream, but her reservoir of strength seemed empty. Occasionally her opening eyes encouraged a partial smile on her lips. Powerless to help, Sabuer was devastated. He began to look at his life and the way in which misfortune had surrounded it. He had hoped his achievements at college would be a source of pride, like that day when he had been registered and people from all over the village had gathered in numbers celebrating with Mars Farkinson the gift she had always wanted. How happy they were then. But her illness had blighted any such celebration, leaving only sadness. He lay on the bed beside her, hugged and kissed her, but there was no response. Her lack of movement hurt him the most and both he and Griff wanted to die in her place, but unfortunately life did not work that way.'

'Where is the doctor?' he asked. 'Surely he could do something for her?'

Someone answered; it could have been Mrs Fagan. 'She has already been taken to see the doctor and he could do little for her. We can only make her comfortable until she is ready to die.'

Those words ripped into Sabuer's heart and soul. He had just got used to a having a Mum who had taught him how to live. Two more years and he could have given her anything. Wealth, pride, love and grandchildren; the things that make a mother feel proud. There was no point in going back to college, he thought. She might not live to see or enjoy any of it. Sabuer decided there and then he would stay at home and savour every moment of his Mum's and Papa's lives.

Knowing she could die at any given time he held her hand and said his goodbye. The comforting words he spoke aloud could not save her from dying. She weakened with every passing day. It was surprising to Sabuer that she lasted as long as she did; she had no strength to move or speak. She lay in bed as though she was wait-ing to hear something special, but what, he wondered? Minutes dragged into to hours and the day seemed to last forever. Time stood still and no one could plan for tomorrow. But he could hear her voice ringing in his head saying, 'I will make sure you can read, write and speak.' What could he promise her, he wondered. 'She is dying, so what is her greatest achievement?' he asked himself. Then it clicked in his head. Her school, of course.

Lying beside his mother, tears flooding his eyes, he gently whispered, 'I am now a qualified teacher, Mum, and I promise you that I will keep your schoolchildren well educated for as long as I live.'

Mrs Farkinson opened her eyes as though in shock and gave the most beautiful smile he had ever seen, sending relief to the hearts of those around her bed. They thought she was about to recover, but it did not last; she closed her eyes never to open them again. She had waited all those weeks for his promise. How wonderful it is to die knowing that you have accomplished all that you have worked for.

During the vigil people had agonised over her impending death and prepared themselves for it, but when it happened everything altered. Nothing could have prepared them for how they felt. No one was left untouched. Sabuer looked at his Papa, wondering whether he, too, was thinking of leaving him. Their broken spirits embraced and silently they promised to care for each other. The atmosphere in their home felt like the aftermath of a category seven tornado that had destroyed everything in its path. A once tranquil house became a place of sorrow, a place of grief for the loss of one so dear.

The Farkinson family had given love in everything they had done and so were never short of friendly faces. Their home had been a centre for advice, especially for those who suffered abuse and degradation at the hands of their master or elders. Mrs Farkinson had always been there with a listening ear and comforting words and sometimes a solution to their fears. The news of her death brought people out in droves to pay their respects to a priceless lady they could never forget.

Within three days her funeral was organised and on the afternoon of the third day, her burial took place. Neither Griff nor Sabuer were allowed to take any part in those planning. At the beginning of her illness, while she had still been in control and Sabuer was still at college, she had arranged it all: which songs to sing, which bible readings to read, the time and place she was to be buried. She was a gifted lady who knew and accepted death as part of the cycle by which life revolves. The funeral was a massive occasion with dignitaries attending from all walks of life; the Governor, nobility, police, army and navy, politicians, and people from near and far, but, most importantly, the children of her school, young and old. Her interment was the most talked about celebration of a passing life that the island had ever witnessed. Those who had gone on to become professionals in their chosen careers cherished fond memories of her energy as a teacher. They were forceful in their praises; driven by gratitude their words inspired Sabuer to make the school his Mum had founded a permanent memorial. It would be the best school in the Caribbean in her honour. From a classroom of four children to the hundreds that attended at the time of her death, she had built that school.

However, over the following weeks of grief, Sabuer's will to keep the promise he had made began to wilt. His brain was filled with reasons why he should not leave his Papa and devote all his energy to the school. Most daunting of all was the prospect of having to follow in his Mum's footsteps. People had declared her the best, so how could he do her memory the justice it deserved, he wondered.

As time went on, and people settled back into their daily routines, parents became unhappy with the progress of their children's education. It was not as good as it once was, they shouted. The school needed leadership; someone as dedicated as Mrs Farkinson whose superb teaching skill had been inspirational to her pupils. Their messages spurred Sabuer into action and shamed him into fulfilling the dreams of both his mothers; Sabuer's Mum, who had given him a purpose to live, and Lafty's mother who had wanted an education for her son. It also fused in his mind the thought of seeing his biological mother again and made him wonder if she was alive or dead.

Armed with a message to deliver, Sabuer marched to the school and, without there being an advertised vacancy, he requested the post, saying he wanted to transform the teaching results. The school was governed by several bodies; the church, police, the magistrate and the plantation owner. And luckily, on the day he chose to arrive, that body of people was already at the school having a meeting to examine the parents' complaints. He approached the group, whom he knew individually and put his case forward in the same manner as his Mum had done the day she had presented his case to the magistrate and registered his presence on the island.

They all listened, agreed he was the best person for the job and gave him the post to improve standards in their school. Sabuer had been given the opportunity he had sought and made the start he had promised. He returned home that day and found his Papa sitting in his Mum's favourite rocking chair, wondering if his son had bitten off more than he could chew. His Papa knew before he was told that his boy had got the job and was delighted. 'Go for it, my son,' said Griff, 'and do your Mum proud.'

Sabuer was pleased to hear those words, knowing that he would not feel he had let her down.

CHAPTER 15

Dreams Fulfilled

Sabuer spent his first year reorganising the school, setting new targets and goals to achieve. He had requested more buildings for extra classroom space, which were quickly put in place, and divided large classes into smaller, more manageable sizes. During this period of grief, and reorganisation of the school, and time spent caring for his Papa, he had a reply to one of his many letters of enquiry about the shipwreck that had brought him to the Island.

The letter confirmed that there had been a shipwreck at the time he had stated, ten years ago. It also stated the ship's owner and its captain, but there was no mention of any of the names of the crew. The letter went on to say, 'Your biological mother might still be alive and would be living in the town where you were born.' That was the most exhilarating news he had had in the ten years.

To make matters worse, the letter had been brought to him by the girl with whom he had fallen in love on the very first day he had seen her at that very same school. As she had handed him the letter, she had said, 'Yes, I will marry you.' Her words stopped him in his tracks but were not unexpected. She had become his rock throughout the devastating times of his Mum's illness and right up to her death. Through thick and thin, endless days and nights crying and grieving, she had stood beside him with comforting words in his ear. The fact that she was a teacher working at the school had helped to maintain their close relationship.

Sabuer had asked her to marry him while at university but he had not been prepared for her answer right at that moment. 'You ask for a drop of rain,' he thought, 'and the next thing you know, it buckets down.'

His mind was all over the place, and for few days he could not make a rational decision. If only his Mum were alive she would know what to do in a situation such as his. But she was dead and both he and his Papa were grieving and it was not the right time to make any decision on marriage. Furthermore, though he clearly loved his girl, the purpose of marrying her and taking on the responsibility of a family was partly to fulfil his parents' expectation. What was the point of getting married, he wondered. His Mum would not be there to organise the wedding and make it special. He did not think he could marry without his Mum's presence.

However, his twenty-fourth birthday was fast approaching. He had become a grown man whose daily decisions were based on responsible and informed knowledge. He had received a good grounding from well-balanced parents whose worldly knowledge had equipped him and steered him in the right direction. It was time he had an adult talk with his Papa, he thought, to explore what they both wanted for each other. Marrying his girlfriend was precisely what he wanted. With him being a family man and them both being teachers, it would be the base for a perfect partnership that could quickly shake up the school. He was also desperate to see the biological mother that he truly loved, but terrified to leave the man who had save his life. They had become increasingly close; closer than he'd ever been to Ruben, his natural father. And with good reason. Griff was more important to Sabuer than the need to leave the island or to get married. He believed that if his attention was focused on anything other than his Papa, he might go as his Mum had gone. After all, Griff was always talking about meeting his Mum beyond the grave in another life.

Sabuer needed the help of his closest friend and surrogate mother, Mrs Fagan. She had known his Mum as well as he had and could be objective in any decision making. But he needed more than mere advice. Although he was reaching twenty-four he had no experience in how to make a girl happy. He had always been too busy studying for his career instead of experimenting with the unknown. To the unsuspecting eye he was an educated person. It should not have been difficult for him to know how he felt towards this girl and for him to allow his intelligence to guide his actions. But it would have been inexcusable had he taken those feelings to his Papa, as regardless of his experience, it was far too delicate a subject. Though he was truly in love, they had not intimately confirmed their feelings. Those were not the sort of discussions he wanted to have with his Papa, purely through respect, but, more importantly, he had to avoid the slightest hint that could lead to his Papa feeling he was unloved or was being left out. Any suggestion of marriage or travel to see his biological mother could spark those feelings. Mrs Fagan would be the right person to speak to his Papa and prepare his thoughts. She had been a friend to his parents all their lives, and was qualified in every way. Even though his Papa knew his girlfriend, had accepted her into the family and felt they would get married at some stage, he was grieving. Any inappropriate statement might cause feelings of worthlessness and rejection. Sabuer's surrogate mother Mrs Fagan was the ideal person to fill the void his Mum had left, and arrange any future marriage, travel, or otherwise.

An impenetrable bond had been woven between them over the years that had created a trust that rivalled that with his Mum. He had told her his secrets; how he felt about Greta, and she had been aware from the start of their relationship. However, he had informed her of the news of his biological mother. He had mentioned only that he would like to trace his family tree. He had also told Mrs Fagan of his intention to marry Greta but that he did not know how and where to start; nor did he want his Papa to become concern.

Mrs Fagan sat and carefully listened to this emotionally charged young man and was willing to do whatever was required of her.

Sabuer knew that at sometime he would have to explain the plan he had for his Papa, but not until they were accepted by his future wife.

Three months later, Mrs Fagan had spoken to Griff and prepared him for the moment when Sabuer was ready to explain his plans and begin the preparation for his wedding day. It had been three years since his Mum's death and the emptiness he felt was ever-present. But as the saying goes, 'Living comes before dying.' He was constantly encouraged not to forget her, but to leave the past behind and get on with life. Sabuer had to decide what was more important; continuous grieving or embracing his love for his girl-friend and Papa. The school was doing fine; parents were happy with the improvement in their children's education. His hard work had paid off while his girlfriend waited.

He arrived home one evening to find his Papa sitting on the porch in his wife's rocking chair, as though she was there and they were having one of their usual conversations. Sabuer knew at a glance that his Papa was up to something, so he went and sat beside him. 'How was your day Papa?'

'I am fine, son, and what kind of day did you have?'

'The usual, Papa. Teaching shouting children who want to learn.'

'That is good, son, your mother used to say the same when she got home.'

'I remember it well, Papa. But she was always happy?'

'Are you happy, son?'

'Yes, Papa. Do I look sad?'

'Not when you are smiling, which you are always doing.'

'I'll always smile for you, Papa.'

'Is there something on your mind, son?'

'You know me too well to hide anything from you. Yes, Papa, there is something I'd like to tell you, and I hope you'll be pleased for me.'

'What is it, son? The suspense is killing me!'

'I am thinking of getting married.'

'Who to, son?'

'To Greta, Papa. I love her and I know you like her too. Who knows, Papa, maybe one day soon you might get grandchildren.'

'That is the best news I've had for a long time. When is the big day, son?'

'We haven't planned the date as yet, Papa. We just want to know if you are happy with our decision.'

'Happy? Did you say happy, son? I am ecstatic. If your mum was here, she would be over the moon. But she is not, so I'll have to play her part.'

'That's alright, Papa, we don't want you to do anything, other than to enjoy the day and yourself.'

'Okay, my son, I will. I certainly will.'

No further explanation was needed and Griff went from the house skipping like a five-year-old child with his first toy, eager to share the news with his friend Desney and others, leaving Sabuer a very happy young man.

It was strange the way things evolved that evening, as though Griff had been expecting Sabuer to say what he had. Earlier, Griff had cooked a feast-like dinner for his son, as though he was preparing to celebrate good news. The table had not been so beautifully laid since his wife's death. She had been the fussy one, who liked to see the dinner table inviting a healthy appetite. The element of surprise had unbalanced his thoughts. His appetite for food had disappeared and he could not eat a morsel. Whether it was the thought of the wedding and the role he had to play, or the possibility of grandchildren to fully enrich his life, it had an immediate effect on him. His thoughts turned to massive changes. From that moment, Griff became a different person. Fun and laughter became his daily routine, something which gave his friends much to talk about.

Sabuer was a predictable person, level-headed, who saw things rationally, but he too became as fidgety as his Papa. Overcoming his fears, he had talked to his Papa, explained his plans, but this had somehow set his nerves on edge. He could not sit still, nor could he concentrate on his after-school work marking papers, so he went in search of Greta. Her presence, he thought, would make him calm. She lived approximately two miles away, which would normally be an hour's walk. However, that evening it was doubtful that his feet touched the ground. He was bursting with completion. His father's reaction had been just as he had been hoping for. The news was too exciting to keep to himself. He needed his closest partner to share in that happy hour.

Sabuer had lost his Mum but had gained a surrogate mother in Mrs Fagan, and he could be thankful for the work she done in preparing Papa for that satisfying acceptance. The dreaded obstacle had been removed and he could get on with his plans, knowing that Papa would not become fearful of any decision he made.

Sabuer and Greta made a great couple. There were just a few weeks between their birthday and they had grown up maintaining that friendly respect for each other that had been apparent from the day they had met as children in the school yard. She was the daughter of the village police sergeant, whose position earned him great respect. His approach to his work had resulted in a well-structured community with little or no lawlessness. Greta was his only child and he guarded her interests much as he guarded his prison cell. Sabuer was somewhat fearful of him, but the passing years saw their friendship grow and saw the policeman become no different to his father Ruben. Both men had similar attitudes, always too busy with their work and others, and spending less time with their families.

Sabuer and Greta had no idea at first that they would grow up and fall in love, nor that they would be willingly planning their wedding, but they were a match made in heaven. She was a very lovely young lady whose energy was devoted to the building of a good community; fitting the daughter-in-law's role in a way that would have suited Mrs Farkinson wishes. Sabuer, on the other hand, was the very best that any parent could expect of a young groom. He was educated, with impeccable behaviour and commanded respect to match, qualities that made the police sergeant happy to endorse their union. The pair had been dignified throughout their courtship, and this had won them a lot of respect. Though they had talked about marriage, they had been fearful of Griff's reaction and no time had been fixed. Yet, when Griff had been told his delight had been beyond measure, which made those worrying years seem in vain. Griff had told Sabuer that, upon his death, the family home would become his, so it would be his right to bring home his wife and complete the family.

The village buzzed as everyone saw themselves party to a celebration, whether or not they were invited. As a matter of fact, there were no specially written invitations. The villagers were an extended family. Their lives had been touched by the Farkinsons, whose skills and dedication had helped to build the place in which they lived. This was a once in a lifetime challenge they were willingly gearing up for. Sabuer's colourful lifestyle had become the focal example to the people of their forgotten fishing village; his presence compelled the plantation masters to recognise the boy that had once been overlooked. He was as important to each individual as their own child. He was marrying the daughter of the most feared person in the village, the police sergeant. And she was wedding the teacher's son. There was no expense spared; new suits and frocks for everyone, which put a massive strain on the tailors and dressmakers.

Though Mrs Fagan was getting on in age, she was quite capable of organising the celebration that everyone was looking forward to. Filling the void of Mrs Farkinson she saw herself as being no different to Sabuer's mother. Three months passed quickly and the wedding day arrived. The preparations had been superb. Griff and the policeman were in awe at its splendour. As both fathers proudly stood by their son and daughter, they each admired the implacable choice their child had made. Restricted by emotions, both men were left speechless.

The horse-drawn carriage bore an immaculate sheen, enhanced by the platted leaves of coconut palm that created heart-shaped arches, forming the sign of love. The budding flowers of water lilies, delicately hung in nests of bells, complemented the spectacle of well-groomed horses, and completed a stunning picture. It was a fitting tribute to a perfectly matched couple. People travelled for miles to see and share in an exhibition of the like that had never before been seen. It was the setting of a new trend that opened the eyes of the country folk. They came alive as they lined the narrow road leading to church, occupying every vantage point around its ragged edges, while others looked on from every available position. With two only carriages for the wedding party, guests filed behind. Bursting at its seams, the little church was immersed in the glory of a sunny day, while the echoing chimes of its peeling bells vibrated the landscape.

The ceremony was conducted by the mission preacher, whose duties continued at the reception hall with the blessing of the feast and their cake. Thank God they did not have far to go; only a few hundred yards to school hall, where the celebration took place.

Some said the wedding was a society affair and so it should be, as everyone had done their best to arrive in style just as Mrs Farkinson would have done. It could not have happened to a nicer couple. A long, drawn out evening of colourful speeches followed; some were rich and meaningful, others were comedic. All joined in with the spirit of the day. Food and drink was in plentiful supply. There was enough for everyone to enjoy with a lot left over for guests to take home for others who could not attend. It would appear that half the country was in attendance. People were puzzled as to where all the food had came from. But then neither the police sergeant nor the Farkinsons were poor. Sabuer and Greta had become the newest

Mr & Mrs Farkinson. It was the happiest day in both their lives; everything had turned out precisely the way their parents had hoped.

After an exciting evening, Sabuer and Greta returned to their matrimonial home where she became the younger Mrs Farkinson, another teacher to generate life and herald a new beginning for Griff and Sabuer. There was no such thing as a honeymoon, so they set about restructuring the house, making their own stamp of identity on what had become their future. The wedding took place on a Sunday, which meant they could stay at home for one whole week and get know each other better. They did not have a photographer to snap their wedding pictures, but they got the next best thing; a painter painted their wedding portrait, a present from her father.

Sabuer, the boy from a distant land, the poorest place on earth, had suffered the pain of a disabling world but had been restored by nature's redressing balance, which allowed him to enjoy what had seemed an impossible dream. His mother's dreams were finally fulfilled, and it was left to him to ensure that those like him would never give up. It was also a time to reflect on the damage the human race caused and how nature's unique recycling methods have a habit of repairing the broken bits. Although he had lost two mothers, he had a wonderful wife.

CHAPTER 16

Nature Resolve

Happiness grows like water lilies, with a fragrance that keeps replenishing the feeling of freshness. The villagers had been wonderfully happy the day Sabuer and Greta had married, and the more they reflected on the wonder of that day the stronger their feeling grew Sabuer was a miracle boy. Why had so many good things happened in their village since he had arrived? It was a question he could not answer, nor did he want to find an answer; he was very happy with his wife and the lifestyle they lived.

With Greta by his side, their vision to make their school the best in the country was being fulfilled, as pupil after pupil returned encouraging exam results. In his enthusiasm to succeed he took the school into a massive improvement programme which was quickly given roaring approval and the school progressed accordingly. There was also good news from expected and unexpected sources. Having been in touch an old friend from the place where he had been born, he had received another letter. His friend was the slave child whose mother had been cook at the plantation house, the good lady that gave his mother Marybell food to feed them as children. Sabuer's friend was the son of the plantation boss and had been given an education. His friend, Joseph, knew the whereabouts of his mother and sister and could give accurate information. Joseph's letter confirmed that Marybell was alive and was living with her daughter Celene. It was shattering news for Sabuer, knowing that he had taken the decision not to leave Griff and travel outside the country. However, Sabuer shared the news with his wife and told her the full story of his life, or what he could remember. He had asked Greta not to repeat a word of it to Griff or the Fagans, and to keep their correspondence private, but the flow of letters between Sabuer and Joseph continued. He would sometimes send Joseph gifts of money for his mother, until such time as it was possible to see her. Nothing was said to his Papa or to Mrs Fagan.

Two years of marriage blessed them and Greta became pregnant with their first child. The Farkinson family was about to take a massive stride forward. It was the sort of news everyone had waited for with bated breath. Once again there was this feeling that every villager was a part of Sabuer's and Greta's life. The happiness they generated within their village rapidly spread across the land, creating pride among families whose children were being taught by either the mother of the miracle boy or the man himself. While the villagers celebrated, Greta accepted the precious gift of childbirth. There was a moment of pain, then elation at having fulfilled her marriage vows. She gave birth to a son, a well-desired prize for her husband, and a grandson for her father the policeman and Griff. It was the second most exhilarating time for the families and villagers.

It was extra special for Griff. He had lost the compulsion to grieve, and gained the energy to celebrate. Griff was looking forward to meeting his wife, albeit it in another life. He had so many interesting stories to tell her; the wonderful time he had had in seeing their son get married, and their first child being born in the house they had built.

For a while Griff was overwhelmed with excitement and could not get his priorities in any order. One minute he was talking about his wife, and within the flash of an eye lid he was busy planning activities he hoped to accomplish with his grandson. Whatever schemes he was dreaming up for his grandson, all that mattered to

Sabuer and Greta was that Griff was happy. The young couple seemed content to take a back seat and allow their fathers to dominate their achievements.

They had all agreed to name the baby after Sabuer's would-be grandfather, Elaina Farkinson's father Alexander. Griff was very pleased that Sabuer had accepted the name because he was very fond of his father-in-law whom knew very well had been a good and decent man. Any decision that would preserve his memory was a good thing. The young Mrs Greta Farkinson and the old Mrs Elaina Farkinson both held an unrivalled position of respect within the community. Their work had involved the teaching of children and the building of a better equipped community, and their reputation was known in every home for miles around. When Greta gave birth to her child, the joy the community felt was infectious.

It was the custom then that well-respected mothers were not allowed to do any physical work for three months after giving birth, especially for the first time. Everyone wanted to help in one way or another. Some elected to carry out the washing, some the clearing, others the cooking. In all their reaction created more willing hands than actual work. But there were rules to fellow, which had to be carried out in an orderly manner, and no one was better placed to see it through than Mrs Fagan. Her knowledge was invaluable in maintaining the high standards of the Farkinson home which would have been her best friend's priority had she been alive.

Sabuer was working twice as hard. He had to cover his wife's classes and see to the administration of a smooth-running school. And if that was not enough, young Alexander cried relentlessly during the nights and kept him awake. Happy though he was for this bundle of joy, the lack of sleep was taking its toll, and he began to look as tired as he felt. Nevertheless, the sheer accolade of becoming a father sent his heart pumping ten to the dozen. He could hardly wait to get home at the end of a gruelling day.

Griff sat on the porch and watched his son. He was trying to skip along the pathway as he usually did; but he had difficulty lifting those tired legs. Griff had never been the father of an infant and was lacking the experience. He wondered if his son had bitten off more than he could chew but on many occasions he was told by his friends how happy they were. 'Nights are for babies,' they said. 'They never stop crying.'

After a few weeks of this madhouse affair Mrs Fagan was called to the rescue. Her stay lasted two weeks, during which she slept with baby Alexander and calmed his crying, which was a surprise to everyone but sheer joy to Greta, Sabuer and Griff. Mrs Fagan set the agenda for young Alexander. All that was left to do was for them to follow her instructions. But Griff was the worst of all the adults. He had never before slept in the same house as a baby and was nervously worrying that the child was very ill, possibly going to die. Griff would not sleep when the others did and stayed wake listening for Alexander's cries. He did not have to worry. Mrs Fagan comforted the baby, sending him to sleep as babies should sleep.

Sabuer was thankful for a peaceful rest. Very soon, he thought, his routine would return to some sort of order. Greta had no fear. She knew that her baby was healthy and took each day as a learning curve. She was the calmest of the three, and kept her husband and father-in-law in check. Soon the little man had settled down and was happily taking food. There was no more crying and Griff could sleep. So could his father Sabuer, whose hurried steps along the pathway got quicker by the day as he rushed home to see his son and wife.

The passing months saw the little man grow steadily. Soon it was time for Greta's return to the classroom full of wondering minds, leaving an open vacancy for a nanny. Gathering women prepared themselves to fill the post that they each saw as their own. Once again Mrs Fagan stepped into the breech, but this time she had to take a back seat as age was against her. The demanding cares of a baby, five days per week, were too big a responsibility to place on her shoulders. The job needed a younger person, but Mrs Fagan wanted to choose that person, and she already had her favourite candidate ready and waiting.

Returning to the classroom where she had been badly missed was a tough challenge for Greta to face. Though the sparkling eyes and brilliant white teeth of the smiling faces of her pupils lit up the classroom, her heart was saddened. She had left her child in someone else's care, a situation that was difficult to accept. She loved the sounds and smells of the classroom but loved her child a lot more. Mrs Fagan tried on many occasions to prepare her for that day but Greta did not understand the emotions involved until she walked through those classroom doors. She needed time and the comfort of a loving husband to restore her innate peace. That day became the longest in her life and she could not wait for it to end, so that she could get away and hug her baby boy.

Griff and Mrs Fagan were there to remind her that love had not ceased because she was absent. And slowly, as the days passed and she found her way gradually back into the joy of teaching, she became happier and her fears subsided. At the end of each day, she arrived home to the welcome smiles of a happy child. Alexander had begun to carve his identity, but he knew his mother, his father and those that cared to make his life comfortable.

However, amid this happiness, nature followed its course. The heavens opened each day; the rain became heavier, flooding the landscape and the whirling wind increased in strength. Panic started spreading in the minds of those who hoped the rain would not be prolonged. The rain and wind prevented the fishermen from going out to fish, forcing them to wait for calm. And in the middle of the night, while they slept, disaster struck.

The island experienced one of its most horrific storms. Like a thief in the night the storm destroyed all within its path, taking the lives of many friends and injuring countless others. The storm smashed the home of Griff's best friend Desney, killing him outright. It wrecked the Fagans' home, leaving them homeless and injured Mrs Fagan, but they were among the lucky ones. They had two children who lived on the other sheltered side of the island who came and took their parents to live with them. The Fagans were two old people, now, too frail to rebuild and start again, and the storm signalled the end of a beautiful family relationship that had been priceless to both the Farkinson and the Fagan families. Unfortunately, the Fagans did not live to see Alexander grow up. Within one year one of arriving at their new home, and two months between each other, they died. Years of joyful happiness turned to endless days of sorrow and loss. The death of the Fagans took with it the history of Sabuer's life on the island, as he could remember it, and for him nothing could ever be the same.

Half the villagers suffered a similar fate, and with many so poor it was doubtful if they could ever rebuild what they had lost. It was a sorrowful sight as the school was turned into shelter at night and a classroom for the surviving children in the day. Whether it was luck or another miraculous intervention the Farkinsons' home was left intact. Griff was a careful man who took pride in his home and kept his house in good repair, maintaining its strong robust structure so that it was capable of withstanding a gale force wind. That could have the reason why our house was saved and not another miracle as many would like to believe.

Though the community was exposed to this veil of sadness, there was a ray of hope. The sun did not suddenly stop shining and there was energy among the living; more so at the Farkinsons' house, where they had a little baby boy who reminded them of life's cycle and brought smiles to lighten their darkened thoughts.

Sabuer and Greta's workload became twice its normal burden as they were alive to their responsibility to the community and to the school. Sabuer also kept up his correspondence with his friend Joseph in Panama. Joseph was up to date with the new baby, the storm and the deaths. And Sabuer was in touch with news of Marybell and her family. She had received his gift and was very grateful.

Losing his Mum and surrogate mother and reading Joseph's letters made Sabuer yearn to see Marybell again, so much so that he began to experience feelings of repentance and at one point sought God's forgiveness. He felt he had done his mother wrong when he had thought badly of her while on board the ship as a child.

As the storm-hit villagers patched up their lives, Alexander had developed and granted the wishes of Griff, his grandfather. Griff was given the opportunity to walk and play with his grandson, something his grandmother would have loved. It broke the child and his young family when Griff died seven years after his wife, leaving his four-year-old grandson and a dedicated son and daughter-in-law to mourn his loss. He was truly missed even though his death was not unexpected. He had longed to be reunited with his wife and his death was the vehicle for that journey. He had lived a fulfilled life and had had his wishes for a son and grandson granted. It gave Sabuer a sense of pride knowing that his Papa, a good man, had been given the chance to live his dreams.

With Alexander's fifth birthday fast approaching there was no sign of any other children. The dust began to settle and Sabuer felt he wanted to see his biological mother again, and for her to know his family. He knew from Joseph's letters that she was alive and living with her daughter and two children. He also knew that their lifestyle was not as poor as he could remember it being. His sister had married one of the plantation bosses which had put the family in a good position to maintain a decent lifestyle. The thought of seeing her was getting too strong to contain and his only release was to make the journey. Whether or not his losses were affecting his mind, it was not clear, but Greta was not going to stand in the way of her man's wishes.

So Greta took time out from her class and went to the travel agent and booked a passage for all the family on a four-day journey across the Caribbean waters. Sabuer needed a rest, she thought. He had not had a day off work since the death of Papa, and a trip would give him some quality time with his son and fulfil his greatest wish.

Sabuer got home feeling tired and dejected. Greta sat beside him brandishing her usual smile and told him what she had done and why she had had to miss her class. 'I went and booked our passage today, on a steam ship bound for Panama. You will be able to see your mother.' Sabuer, the man who always exercised rational thinking, burst into tears, and it was clear to Greta that her husband had taken his loss far worse than he had pretended. She could only hope that the trip might hold the key to him becoming his own self again.

There were five days of anxious waiting while Sabuer made the house secure and Greta packed their clothes. Though she was not the same size as her mother-in-law, she brought a dress that could be altered to fit. That would a beautiful present, she thought. Sabuer's school was on holidays which meant he was free to enjoy himself if he could and everyone was willing him to do just that. Sabuer was again terrified at the prospect of sailing; it was a fear of which he would probably never be rid.

The day of their departure came and everything was in order. The giant ship had anchored in the bay while the shuttle boats ferried goods and passengers for boarding. They stepped from the house to a waiting crowd, who cheered Sabuer on towards his deserved break, though no one in the crowd knew the truth of his journey. With helping hands to carry the luggage the short walk was done with relative ease. The tiny harbour came alive and for a moment it was easy to think that a member of the royal family was present rather than a simple school teacher. Greta was first to climb the ladder and stepped inside the shuttle boat, followed by Alexander being carried by one of his godfathers. Sabuer smiled and tightly grabbed the railing of the shuttle boat as it rolled from side to side and sent his heart pumping much faster. Thoughts of that disastrous night swamped his brain. He was dying inside but could not say so, and had to clown his fears with a smile. The little boat skimmed the surface water bouncing like a rubber ball as

Sabuer's smile hid his phobia. A five minute journey seemed to last a thousand years before the little boat was carefully pulled up alongside the giant vessel. Nervously, they climbed the rocking steps that danced to the movement of an angry ship, where men in white checked their papers and showed them to a cabin three decks below, a terrifying prospect for four long days. Throughout the journey, Sabuer took himself to the upper deck twice a day to have his meal; the rest of his journey time was spent lounging in his cabin.

CHAPTER 17

Mere Dream

Arriving in his homeland, a place Sabuer thought he would never again see, was an emotional rollercoaster that seemed endless. Walking down the steep steps leading onto solid ground, he held his son tightly to his chest while his wife followed closely. They walked through the shed-like buildings, flanked by sailors and officials, some from the ship, others from the island's security. This elegantly postured black man, whose proud steps had captured their attention, was the centre of their focus as he and his family approached the official desks. Who could this black person be? They were not going to take any chances. After all, a black person was not regarded as someone of importance. So the teacher and family man was extensively questioned by the police and immigration services. The colour of his skin had created an immediate suspicion that this innocent man and his family were runaways and up to no good. The officials wanted to know everything about Sabuer and his family. Thank God they were teachers, and respected members of their society. It took a few hours and a full explanation of the reason for their visit before the officials were satisfied and they were allowed to collect their luggage.

Sabuer and his family filed to the front of an open building where they were met by the staring eyes of many people waiting. Reaching the end and touching the hands of welcoming faces, it hit him. How would he know his mother? Would she look the same, he wondered? Many years had passed and his mental picture was blurred. It was then that he remembered he should listen for the name Lafty, in case she had forgotten his new name, Sabuer.

It was not long before he heard the name Lafty being shouted. He could see this little lady but could not imagine it was his mother Marybell. At first he had ignored the shouts and looked for his friend Joseph. From his letters, Sabuer had a fairly good idea what Joseph looked like, but still the name Lafty echoed. Then he heard someone shout, 'Saba.' His body came alive. The shouts were those of his mother who he had seen in the distance, but could not recognise. The crowded forecourt was noisy, dirty, dusty and very smelly, with people moving in all directions, humping bags, baskets and bundles of wood. In fact every known article was being carried from one place to the other. Sabuer and Greta pushed and shoved towards the echoing call, waving their hands to attract attention and at last they reached the small lady and her daughter, behind who stood his friend Joseph hidden by this massive bundle on a horse drawn cart.

Sabuer ran to the woman and it became clear that she was indeed his mother. All those years he had not taken into account that she would have aged. Her once smooth skin had wrinkled and dried, and her long straight hair was short and greying, and she seemed to have shrunk many sizes from the mother in his memories. Nevertheless, she was his mother and he loved her even more because her decision to send him away had made him an educated and wealthy man. He could not wait until they got home; he was eager to tell her the story of how he had reached the island of his home. Greta was taken aback at his urgency. Did he think his mother might die before they reach her home, she wondered?

Starting with the storm and the shipwreck, Sabuer told it all. How the man who had found him had taken him home to his sick wife, who was a teacher. How they had registered him in their name because he could not speak clearly at the time. And how they had given him the name Sabuer because by the time he could speak to tell them his real name it had been too late. He described how everyone had seen him as the miracle child, and treated him as such and how he had kept both the secret and their dreams in tact.

'They knew I had a mother but had no idea who she was, or where she lived, and it was their greatest desire to have a child in their lives. So I enjoyed what I thought was the adventure that you had wanted for me. I would still be enjoying it, but I did not want to continue living this happy lifestyle knowing that you were alive and that I could not see you. I especially wanted you to see the outcome of your decision.'

Joseph could not get a word in as both mother and son competed to inform each other of their passing experiences. He was a fairly wealthy man with a modern horse drawn cart and, as he had said, a large farm with many workers, who were probably working in slavish conditions. They had boarded the cart and off they went on a journey that took just over an hour. Things had changed in twenty years and Sabuer was delighted at the many houses that had sprung up along the narrow winding road. Joseph pointed out the spot where he once lived with his uncle and his family.

'They have all gone,' he said.

'Where are they now?' Sabuer asked.

'Your uncle bought a large farm deep in the countryside and took the entire family with him.' Joseph replied.

The landscape was more beautiful than Sabuer could remember. With fields of corn, sugar cane and wheat, the vastness and variety of crops was not quite what Greta and Alexander were expecting. They were pleasantly surprised. At the top of the hill, Joseph pulled on the reins and the horses stopped, allowing the visiting young family to look out over a breathtaking vista. Stretching into the distance as far as the eye could see, the green fields and tall trees were like the picture on a magnificent postcard, and the sight left Greta in a trance-like state as though she was dreaming. Her facial expression brought comfort to Joseph, Sabuer and Marybell, instilling in them both a peace of mind and a proud sense of achievement. Soon the four giant horses arrived at some steps outside a house and stopped.

'This is where you and your family are going stay, Sabuer. You are my guests.'

'Thank you, Joseph. You must come and visit us next time.'

'I will, Sabuer. I'll take you up on that offer.'

They got off the carriage and went inside the house, which had an elegance they could not compare. The furniture was of the best quality he had ever seen, and could only have been imported, thought Sabuer. Joseph gave them a tour of the house and told them he would take them to Marybell's home the following day. But his excited mother was too anxious to wait as tears of happiness flowed down her cheeks.

'Sit down,' she said. 'Let me look at you just in case you slip from my sight. I don't ever want to forget what you look like. You can look around the house later.'

With the joys of a motherly love bubbling up inside, she proudly hugged her newfound family while her nervous lips trembled uncontrollably.

'I should have given up on you marry years ago, but I could not. Something inside was telling me you were alive, so I waited and waited. Your father turned up three years later. He came to explain the shipwreck and what happened. He also said that no one could find you so, that you were left for dead. They did find Scruffy, his friend, but he was badly injured and lived only a few months. However, his other friend Mud was never found.

'Your father came to apologise for taking you away and worst of all he had no idea if you had lived or died. But even then, having heard that you were more likely dead than alive, my faith remained strong, as if someone was saying to me that you would return. And here you are, with your beautiful wife and a handsome looking grandson. Thank you, God, for giving me my boy back and for helping me to make a decision I was not equipped to make.'

It is amazing what the power of faith can do. The disabling effect of nature in the world in which we live had created a situation Marybell could not resolve. However, with all its disruptive elements, nature's unique stabilising measures were also equipped to solve Marybell's problems. They returned her son to her, along with a daughter-in-law and a grandson, Alexander. They were a family that was educated and could make informed choices, and for her it was the fulfilment of what had been a mere dream.

Marybell's dream did not scar the landscape or create distress to the human race. Nor did it disrupt the delicate balance of nature's stabilising power. Her dream gave hope. And a future generation could take encouragement that both Sabuer's wishes, and the peace of mind Marybell had dreamed of, were granted. If only we could all be as patient.

The Inside Stories Collection

VOLUME 1: